VIC VALENTINE: INTERNATIONAL MAN OF MISERY

Will Viharo

Seattle, WA

VIC VALENTINE: INTERNATIONAL MAN OF MISERY

Copyright 2017 Will Viharo

Front cover art by Matt Brown:
mattbrown22.myportfolio.com
Back cover art and design by Dyer Wilk:
aseasonofdusk.com
Formatting by Rik Hall – WildSeasPress.com

ISBN-10: 0-692-93022-1
ISBN-13: 978-0-692-93022-9

First Printing
Printed in the United States of America

Published by Thrillville Press

www.thrillville.net

To the Writers' Retreat of San Buenas, salud!

Chapter One
SOGGY STYLE

Women don't really think of me as a hunk. More like a chunk. The kind one blows. But I do okay, especially for a guy my age, in my current quasi-professions: full-time dog-walker, part-time detective, on-call gigolo. I'm there for the city of Seattle to fulfill every base need, whether carnal and canine in nature. Vic Valentine, pooch 'n' cooch specialist. *C'est moi.*

I still think about the One That Got Away, though. Well, they *all* got away. Even one of the dogs, which is where this strange saga really begins. But at least I usually got to fuck 'em first—meaning the women—giving us both a memory to cherish, or erase, depending on which side of my boner you were on at the time.

This babe I desperately wanted to nail twenty-five years ago—an impossibly hot Latina named Esmeralda Ava Margarita Valentina Valdez, whom I met on a case back in San Francisco—told me she'd sleep with me only if Donald Trump were magically elected president, which at the time seemed tantamount to Hell freezing over (which itself may never happen now, thanks to climate change). Last I heard, though it's been a while, she was living back in Mexico, probably in direct response to his election, as well as her formerly improbable caveat.

I'm on my way down there now, but it has nothing to do with her. Not directly. I will look her up anyway, if I get the chance, just in case she remembers her end of the bargain, which Trump upheld. I'll give him that much. And the Russians, too. Though I doubt anyone was colluding on behalf of my sex life. It's not exactly a global issue. I am extending its jurisdiction, though, outside the borders of not only my little life, but the entire country of my incidental birth. Expanding my horizons is something a shrink once told me I should try. I don't think he meant it quite so literally, but whatever. It was about time I started exploring south of something other than my own belt.

But before we get there, I need to walk you back a bit, as it were.

Last time I checked in, I was recovering from my latest fiasco, waiting for Mickey Rourke to actually make the movie of my life, an option he took over from this other actor named Charlie, who blew it by becoming implicated in a series of burlesque dancer murders, for which he was proven innocent.

I still had my doubts, but since he let the option of my life story lapse, I no longer felt invested in his fate, except when he was shacked up with my old gal pal Monica Ivy. More on that in a bit.

Anyway, via his agent, with whom I'd signed a contract, I agreed to finally meet Mickey in person nearly two years after he first optioned my life story, in a local Seattle gym, to discuss the movie, and how we'd collaborate on the script.

Let's just say it didn't go so well.

When I got out of the hospital, Monica took me back to my pad in Ballard and nursed me for a while. She was living with a lesbian down in Portland by then, after dumping Charlie, which was a major relief, at least for me.

I considered this a significant trade-up. So did she. Now I wouldn't have to worry about her anymore. Plus I had fresh images to beat off to. I could stop being a private detective once and for all, and follow my true vocation: being a full-time bum.

But then Trump won the election, against all predictions, logic, and reason. The world had gone irrevocably mad. Nothing made sense anymore. Well, it never did to me, so for once, I felt in sync with the chaos around me. I took it in stride. I never had any faith in the fate of humanity, anyway. Now they'd simply escalated their own self-destruction. Good riddance. Sure, they'd take me down with them, since I was a reluctant member of our pathetic species, but so what. I was in my fifties anyway. The clock was ticking faster and faster. I didn't have much to live for anymore. Not that I ever did. Hope never sprang eternal for me. It barely trickled. Now it was nothing but a dried-up well. I did my best to refill it on a regular basis, though. Mostly by pissing in it. I'm a firm believer in recycling. For the good of the planet, of course.

This story—one of revenge, redemption, rejuvenation, and even some random re-animation—really began one early spring day when I was sipping a three-olive dirty Martini expertly prepared by Tara the bartender at my new favorite local hang-out, the Old Fifth Avenue Tavern, right next to Kona Kitchen, another place I frequented for dinner. I normally drank my dinner. My attempts at going stone cold sober had failed, like almost all of my aspirations in life, though I did drink less than I once did. Part of it is because, thanks to Obamacare, I could finally afford a check-up, something I'd been putting off for literally decades. It only finally happened because Mickey Rourke sent me to the hospital anyway, so since I was being treated for various broken parts, they gave me a complete physical. Of course, the results made me immediately regret it. Meaning my access to affordable health insurance, as well as my unpleasant meeting with Mickey. My blood pressure was too high, for one thing, which was no surprise. Also, my "good cholesterol" was too low. In order to balance them both out, I started taking prescription meds. Washed down with booze. I didn't tell the doc that, though.

Anyway, I was getting good exercise these days with my new gig, dog-walking. That's how I discovered the Old Fifth Avenue, while escorting a mutt around the lovely

3

Seattle neighborhood of Maple Leaf. The park over there is beautiful, perfect place to play with pets, flirt with women, and contemplate how sad your little life has become.

I began walking dogs waiting for the movie deal to come through, since I'd burned through most of the cash I made after Monica sold The Drive-Inn down in San Francisco. We were both beneficiaries in the original owner's will, the late proprietor being Curtis Jackson, AKA Doc Schlock, AKA my best friend in the world. When he was alive, anyway. And even a little bit after. Dog-walking also provided me with a way to occupy my time that was relatively productive, and actually useful to someone other than myself.

I was finally content being a bum. In fact, I embraced it. It was too much work to be a punk. I'd failed at that pursuit as I'd failed at most things in life. Now I was just running out the clock, not even waiting for something to happen. It happened anyway, just to fuck with me.

Meantime, I tried not to think about Life or the Universe or that crazy kind of existential jazz too much anymore.

Besides sex, which offered only ephemeral euphoria that immediately evaporated once I ejaculated, I distracted myself from impending doom with pop culture. In addition to my old standby, Frank Sinatra, I was listening to a lot of Leonard Cohen and Tom Waits these days. Their gravelly voices were wizened by hard knocks, sonically soaked in gin and pain, winsome and pensive, poetically tragic, as I egotistically imagined myself. The hard truth? I was an aging Lothario with a pet cat named after my dead best friend, Doc, and now the cat was my best friend. Otherwise, I didn't spend a lot of time with humans, unless it was to fuck one (or vice versa, metaphorically speaking). Pretty soon I'd be dead and it would all be over, anyway. At least for me. The Ultimate Answers will probably disappoint the hell out of me, so why bother to ask? I can wait. Most likely the only thing that awaits us after this brief sprint through a temporal sewer is eternal nothingness, meaning basically way more of the same. For some reason I found that prospect oddly comforting.

Further disorienting my already fragile psyche, some personal favorites from my long, lost youth had magically returned to the popular sphere of consciousness, reassuring me that Time was not an insidious enemy, just a lousy friend that was always late. Blondie had a new album out called *Pollinator; Blade Runner* finally had a sequel; and *Twin Peaks* was in its long delayed third season. Everything old and cool was new and hot again. Except for me. I was somewhere in between. Over halfway-done, and feeling lukewarm.

In addition to music, I rented a lot of movies from Scarecrow Video, the Mecca for lovers of offbeat cinema. I wound up briefly banging one of their cute but snobby hipster clerks. Her name was Rebecca. She had long, stringy red hair, big floppy tits with enormous nipples, and wore very erudite-looking black glasses, which I found so sexy I asked her to leave them on when we were in bed, which she did until I came on them suddenly while she was sucking my cock. It's a bitch to wipe semen off of glasses.

Anyway, I always got the idea I was a pity fuck, though she did appreciate my tastes in obscure, offbeat cinema, which is how we initially hooked up. We loved fucking to 1970s-era Spanish horror movies, especially the ones starring Paul Naschy, or directed by Amando de Ossorio. She was my kind of freak, even if she was something of a film snob.

Despite the hot sex and shared interest in Eurotrash exploitation, it didn't last, not so much because of the age difference (she was in her mid-thirties, I gathered), but because she thought I was an idiot. Or that's my take, anyway. We engaged in these endless geeky debates about pointless movie trivia which she always won. Rebecca was

5

the one who finally informed me that two of my favorite movies, *At Midnight I'll Take Your Soul* and *This Night I'll Possess Your Corpse,* starring José Mojica Marins, AKA "Coffin Joe," were actually in Portuguese, not Spanish, as I'd mistakenly believed since I first watched them back at The Drive-Inn, eons ago.

"But they're *Brazilian* movies," I argued rather smugly.

"Exactly," she said with a rather condescending sigh.

That's when she stopped returning my calls. Then she abruptly quit the store. I still rented movies there, though.

Otherwise I just sat around jerking off. Dog-walking got me out of my house, and sometimes into someone else's bed. That just had to be healthier than never leaving my own. Or so I convinced myself. Once I began placing my own Dog Walker For Hire ads on Craigslist, the floodgates of my loins burst open. And I actually loved dogs, as well as cats. They loved me too, because I distrusted humans almost as much as they did. We could relate.

I met a *lot* of women via this gig. And I don't just mean the clients. Even while walking down the street with any kind of mutt (and I dig all kinds and sizes—my tastes are electric in both dogs and women), almost every passing woman would smile at me. Traffic would literally stop whenever a dog and I wanted to cross the street. Walking dogs in public made me instantly lovable. All I had to do was introduce my dog to a pretty gal, and pretty often she'd introduce me to her pussy. Sometimes I'd meet my prospective date while she was walking her own dog in the park. I'd politely hit on her as our dogs were sniffing each other's asses, which ironically their owners often wound up doing, too. It was easy to get dates this way because I already had something in common with them, being dog lovers, so I could strike up this mutually interesting topic of casual conversation.

Ironically, I had a lot more trouble sealing the sex deal

when I was younger and healthier, though I was actually in better shape in my "fitties" than I was in my "fatties," thanks to my new workout routine. I think that's because I gave up on love and settled for lust, a much more attainable pursuit. In fact, I got laid a lot more routinely as a dog walker than I ever did as a so-called detective.

I should disclose that I'm no longer actually licensed as an investigator. Seattle PD offered to locally reinstate my defunct Bay Area P.I. badge after I saved the city from a pair of serial-killing cops, if only by accident, more or less, but they didn't know that, and that's my *modus operandi*, anyway. But I wound up declining. For one thing, once you have a license to do something, people except you to be, you know, professional and all. Also, while I appreciated their gesture of gratitude, I didn't want to be in cahoots with the cops. I'd learned from hard experience—the only way I learn anything, if at all—to avoid any *quid pro quo* commitments when it comes to law enforcement. They don't practice fair trade, let's leave it that.

I still kept my ancient Corvair, though. It had been through everything with me, going all the way back to my days as a San Francisco private eye, before I migrated northward a couple of years ago, more or less of my own volition, but driven primarily by Fate, my pimp. I love it here, mostly for the soggy weather and dense greenery. But I have to admit, I was having trouble sleeping most nights, at least in my own bed. I was feeling the weight of time crushing what was left of my spirit. My youthful dreams were already long dead. I lived in a state of peaceful resignation. It was called Washington.

Everything changed yet again when a surprisingly well-tanned, curvaceous, middle-aged widower/divorcee responded to my Craigslist ad, asking if I could walk her dog on a semi-regular basis. She left no name, only an address. Turned out she lived over in Wedgwood, on a quiet, tree-lined, sidewalk-free street, in a midcentury modern house, all to herself. I was pleasantly surprised when she opened the door and was wearing nothing but a bathrobe and slippers. She'd just come out of the shower. She looked almost exactly like Dyanne Thorne in *Ilsa, She Wolf of the SS*. With a little Sybil Danning thrown in for good measure. Same sternly sensuous face, impossibly voluptuous body, and big, blond hair. I didn't care if she was an actual Nazi, or even if she tortured me. It had been a while since I'd gotten laid. Well, a couple of weeks, which was quite a stretch by my recent standards.

We got right down to business.

Oddly, during the sex she kept interviewing me, asking me personal questions, like my address, where I liked to hang out, how often I walked dogs, and which routes I preferred. I think I answered all of them, since the heat of passion is like truth serum to me. I was so immersed in her feminine fleshiness she could've gotten anything out of me. For all I knew I gave up my social security number. She could have it. There was never any security in being social anyway, at least not for me.

I had already banged the hell out of Dyanne Thorne's delicious *doppelganger* when I realized she actually *did* have a dog, and the ad wasn't some thinly veiled ruse to elicit the services of a gigolo. I discovered her authentic canine company when it hopped up on her big brass bed while she was making us a drink, and starting licking the pussy juice off my balls. It probably recognized the scent. I'd been lying in bed with my eyes closed, completely drained of seminal fluid, and at first I thought it was "Dyanne" tickling my sticky testicles. She was pretty horrified when she walked in with two Moscow Mules and saw me engaging in casual bestiality with her beloved pet poodle.

"You are a fucking pervert," she said harshly, setting down the copper cups and snatching her precious pup from between my moist, hairy thighs.

"You're the one that tied me up and tortured me, a complete stranger," I said, realizing immediately my retort was weak and ineffectual, especially since the bondage part had been my idea.

Her robe was open and her slightly sagging but still spectacular breasts were exposed, along with her rather hairy bush. She had explained to me that she stayed so tan despite her part-time Seattle residence via regular trips down to a Cabo resort home—a by-product of a generous divorce settlement—where I assumed she was graciously serviced by handsome cabana boys. I got hard again just looking at her. That didn't happen often anymore. But I'd already blown it, however unintentionally. Her poodle started barking at me, like I'd set it up.

Dyanne immediately ordered me out of her house, though I did notice a piece of mail on the way out that revealed her name actually was Dianne Thornton. So I wasn't too far off the mark, after all.

All of this casual sex may seem strange to you, but for me, it was essentially physical therapy. My stomach was perpetually tied up in knots when I wasn't having an orgasm. It was starting to worry me, especially since as I rapidly aged, my sex drive was slowly diminishing. It took longer and longer for me to climax, though once I did, I was like a busted fire hydrant. I was afraid I was literally petering out. No complaints from my patient partners so far, since these delays increased their own chances for satisfaction. I was always great at cunnilingus, mainly due to enthusiasm. I just acquired a taste for pussy early on in life. Now that I was older, I often resorted to eating my way out of actual intercourse, with reciprocal appreciation most of the time, since most of the women I banged were in menopause and their personal oases were gradually drying up, too. Fucking climate change.

Sometimes my talented little tongue—which only got me in Dutch when I used it to talk—wasn't enough, though.

9

Especially if I scored with a screwed-up young college gal with daddy issues I was more than happy to help her resolve via my experienced TLC. Which brings me to the other early link in this chain of unlikely events I'm about to tell you about: a beautiful brunette named Laura, a twenty-something babe I was banging right before I met Dianne. By contrast, Laura had perfect ivory flesh dotted with arty tattoos, jet black hair, and sweet, soft little bosoms, with pierced nipples that often got stuck in my teeth. She reminded me of a young Sherilyn Fenn, at least when viewed via my delusional prism. I thought I was in love with Laura, despite the thirty year age gap. Maybe she had daddy issues, but what were mine? I guess mommy issues. I was never breast fed as an infant. Now I couldn't get enough of the stuff.

I met Laura when she tended bar at Navy Strength, Seattle's fanciest tiki lounge, located down in Belltown. I couldn't afford to drink there on a regular basis, since the cocktails were so pricey, though well worth it if you had the scratch. Anu, the owner, sometime gave me a drink in exchange for walking her dog around the block. But I was mainly there to stalk Laura, with whom I was immediately smitten.

Eventually I figured I'd save money if Laura just made me drinks at home, hers or mine, so I asked her out, or rather, in. We hit it off pretty quickly. Amazingly so, in retrospect, though now I know why, and it wasn't my magnetic personality. But Laura was genuinely sweet to me. Actually, it was Laura who helped me write my first Craigslist pitch for dog-walking gigs, rather than just relying on word-of-mouth. Commercializing my "brand" was all her idea. How could I not love her? She was obviously looking out for my withering welfare, like a sexy nurse in an old folks' home.

The thing is, I often fell obsessively in love with waitresses and female bartenders all over town, of all ages and types, on a fairly routine basis. Even though we had almost nothing in common culturally, I bridged the age gap with my dick, but I could only stretch that so thin. Eventually our lack of common interests, not to mention my geriatric fatigue, always turned them off. I knew I was just a walk on the wild side for them, anyway. Hipster babes liked the idea of seducing a middle-aged private eye, especially one that loved animals. But the novelty wore off after their first four or five orgasms. I couldn't eat my way to their hearts.

One night, Laura actually called 911 when I rolled off her after one brief, intense tussle and had trouble catching my breath. She thought I was having a stroke. No, I assured her through my wheezing. This happens when I stroke myself, too. I wondered what she saw in me.

Then Laura told me I reminded her of her favorite movie character, Austin Powers, because, as she put it, I'm "like this living relic from the past, lost in the wrong time period." Except Mike Myers made those movies about a 1960s secret agent stuck in the 1990s back *in* the '90s. You know, *my* era. Plus I always dressed like a Rat Pack reject from the '60s, Austin Powers' era. Laura had only seen those movies on video because she was just a little kid when they came out in theaters, having been born in 1990. It hurt my head just thinking about it, because for one thing, I suck at math.

Then one day, just like Rebecca, Laura suddenly stopped answering my phone calls, and even quit the bar without notice, the excuse being a "family emergency" that demanded immediate personal attention, though I knew it was because she was afraid I'd die in her bed soon.

Initially, I was devastated. But then I realized that it wasn't the current me that was in love with her. It was the young me, the one I was when I was Laura's age. The poor schnook that was always too eager to fall in love and got attached way too easily, completely alienating girls that were Laura's age back then. I was too needy and desperate. Now that I was old and apathetic, too emotionally burned out to give a damn whether my bold advances were rejected or accepted, I had no trouble scoring with almost any single babe I wanted. If only I still had my youthful energy. I'd wasted it in the vain pursuit of romantic security and domestic bliss.

Despite this belated epiphany, I missed Laura. I even missed Dianne. I thought I'd never see either again. If that were true, none of this would've happened. I still have mixed feelings, but then so were the results.

Now back to the Old Fifth Avenue Tavern. "Drums-a-Go-Go" by the Hollywood Persuaders was playing inside my head as I contemplated my future options while drinking my third dirty Martini. Maybe it was my fourth. In any case, Tara had finally cut me off. Outside, one of my canine clients was tied to a bike rack or something. Maybe it was a parking meter. As long as it was something stationary. I often made these little refueling pit stops during my dog walks. Typically the owners never saw me, and the dogs didn't care as long as they got their Happy Hour treats, too.

Suddenly I noticed what I'd previously assumed had been a bear rug was actually a huge dog lounging on the floor next to one of the booths, beside its owners. I rebooted my blurry vision by blinking my eyes several times. Yup, it was a dog, all right. A *live* one.

"Hey Tara, why didn't you tell me we could bring dogs in here?" I asked. That practice was generally frowned upon in most establishments.

"I did," she replied with a smile. "Every time you come in here."

"Oh." I had absolutely no recollection of those exchanges. Doesn't mean they didn't happen. Most ambient information drifts right by me, even the vocal variety. I'm self-sequestered inside my own head way too much of the time. One reason I made for a lousy detective. One of hundreds.

I grabbed some pretzels from a bowl on the counter and wobbled off my stool and outside to feed 'n' fetch the poor pooch. It had begun to rain pretty hard. In fact, it had been the rainiest winter on record in Seattle, and the deluge was continuing well into springtime. No wonder I was so happy. Plus I was wet on the inside much of the time, too.

At first I panicked because I saw a leash, but no dog. Then I realized the dog was gone.

"Doggone it," I said out loud. But nobody heard me. I figured it—he—must've somehow broken free and wandered off. He couldn't be far, I hoped.

"He" happened to be a black and brown half-Terrier, half-Chihuahua I nicknamed "Little Mickey." As in Rourke. In fact, it was Mickey Rourke's dog. One of them, anyway. Or so I was told by his mysterious, alleged agent, whom I'd never actually met and who never returned my calls anymore, either.

Let me back up a bit and provide some belated exposition (I suck as a storyteller, too): part of my former so-called deal was taking care of this dog for Mickey while he was away shooting our movie. First I ad to "practice," though. In fact, that's how I started thinking about becoming a full time dog walker, anyway, after only doing it here and there for chump change. I'll always be a chump. I'll never change.

But now that he wasn't making our movie, I wasn't sure why I was still obligated to care for the mutt, who actually lived in his own studio loft apartment in Greenwood, with views of both downtown and Mount Rainier. The TV was always left on Cartoon Network, 24/7, and there were movie posters on the wall from *Diner, Angel Heart, The Pope of Greenwich Village, Year of the Dragon, Johnny Handsome, Harley Davidson and the Marlboro Man, The Wrestler*, and *9 ½ Weeks* so the dog would feel at least atmospherically ensconced in his owner's virtual presence. Generally he was cared for by a local biker gang called The Emerald City Wizards, who were on Mickey's payroll, or something. A couple of them were always there on guard duty, drinking beer and smoking weed, paid to simply keep the dog company, though they seemed pretty apathetic toward the little dude. To me they were morose and rude, basically ignoring me whenever I stopped by. I didn't care. Not my problem. My job was simply to walk Little Mickey twice a day, for the sake of exercise and bowel relief. I guess forever. Even though I hadn't heard from Big Mickey in a while, I didn't want to take a chance on simply quitting this gig, even if the contract was now null and void, though it technically hadn't expired yet, so there was that. The bikers gave me an envelope of cash weekly, too. Plus I felt sorry for the dog.

As the rain poured I drunkenly wandered down Fifth Avenue and then up and down the residential side streets, all the way back to Maple Leaf Reservoir Park, where I had been walking him, since we were tired of Greenwood Park back in his own neighborhood. I wish we'd never left. I wish I'd never been born. If I didn't find this dog, his owner would grant that wish retroactively.

I lay on the wet grass sobbing for a while, then hobbled back to the bar, since my Corvair was parked in the lot next door.

That's when I noticed a note inside a plastic bag, tied to the bike rack or parking meter or whatever it was out front. Bleary-eyed, I untied it and took it with me to the car to read:

If you want the dog back, meet me here tomorrow at 6pm. Be alone. Or die.

Then there was an address that was quite familiar to me. For a moment I wondered if expediting the inevitable result of this catastrophe, meaning my sudden demise, might be the preferable option. But then I thought of Little

Mickey, alone with some stranger, who was probably holding him for ransom. I had to save Little Mickey for his sake, not for mine.

What more could possibly go wrong? That's a rhetorical question.

Chapter Two
GOD WITH A BONER

A bit too conveniently, the designated rendezvous point happened to be right around the corner from Little Mickey's studio apartment: the Shanghai Room on Greenwood Avenue, which was adjacent to The North Star Diner, a joint I frequented, down the block from Naked City, a *film noir* themed restaurant/brewery, and up the street from The Lodge Sports Grille, two more of my regular haunts. It struck me as odd that the dognapper would want to meet me so close to Little Mickey's digs, in one of my favorite 'hoods, at one of my favorite hangouts. It made me suspect they knew me, or at least knew about me. I guess my old detective instincts were kicking in. Which meant nothing but trouble for all concerned.

As I drove there in my Corvair, "Drums-a-Go-Go" was still playing inside my head in an interminable loop, even though my Esquivel mix was playing on the car's CD player. In fact, this ancient instrumental stayed with me throughout the course of this entire trip, easily my wildest case yet. If you could even call it a case. You can call me one, anyway.

I know what you're thinking: given the constant complications, why was I still drinking? I mean, wouldn't most normal people realize that stopping for cocktails while walking a dog is just plain stupid, not to mention irresponsible? The answer to that question is simple: Yes. Any normal person would. I don't know what's wrong with me. I really don't.

Definitely, the drink called the North Star Cocktail I

had just ordered at the Shanghai would be my last. For that day. Or at least until my contact showed up.

While mentally ravaging the sexy female bartender, as I always do, I wondered how the dognapper would know I was the one they were supposed to meet. But then I realized: they were already way ahead of me. They knew I was me. Even I didn't know that sometimes.

The Shanghai Room was just my speed and style: a cozily dark dive with first class cocktails, comfy booths surrounding a custom-made horseshoe-shaped bar, and a small corner stage for *karaoke*, something I always avoided at all costs. Christmas lights augmented the festive yet moody atmosphere. There were loquacious barflies right and left of me, obviously regulars. I'd been here several times before but suddenly it was my new favorite bar, especially now that the Old Fifth Avenue Tavern had been tainted by this negative experience.

I'd been there for about half an hour when someone finally tapped me on the shoulder. I turned to see my old pal Dianne Thornton. Her big blond hair seemed even bigger and blonder and her skin even tanner than last time I saw her. Even her tits seemed bigger, and they already loomed large in my fuzzy memory. At first I thought she was my contact, which would've been a real twist in the plot. In fact, "Twin Peaks Twist" by that great Russian surf-lounge band Messer Chups was playing right at that moment on the bar's sound system, successfully drowning out "Drums-a-Go-Go" in my head. But I assumed she just happened to be drinking there the same time as me. I was actually glad to see her.

Then she hauled off and slapped me.

"What the hell?" I said.

"*You're a pervert!*" she exclaimed loudly. The sexy bartender heard that accusation but pretended not to. There went any chance of my scoring with *her*.

"So?" I said.

"You fucked my dog!"

"No, I didn't! He was licking my balls, not the other way around!"

The bartender heard that, too. I wasn't sure I could even drink there again, much less ask her out.

"Want to get out of here?" Dianne said suddenly.

I looked at my watch, sighed, and said, "Sure." I felt embarrassed and worried I'd soon be 86'd anyway. Also, I was blinded by her sun-baked cleavage. Plus I lied to you. I'd had more than one North Star Cocktail. I was resigned to never seeing Little Mickey again. And getting beaten to death by Mickey Rourke. This could be my last hurrah.

We drove in her car back to Wedgwood and then we were naked in her bed. No time to waste at our age. She tied me up and bit, licked, kissed, and sucked me all over. Her dog was barking in the backyard.

But I recognized the bark. It wasn't her dog, or just any dog.

It was Little Mickey.

"Hey, that's not your dog, that's *mine*!"

"I know," she said.

"How do you know?"

"I was the one you were supposed to meet in the bar, dumbass. I left you the note."

"Wait, *really*?" So the plot had twisted back again to my original suspicion.

"I've been following you for weeks. Ever since I saw you last."

"Why?"

"I'm working for someone."

"Who?"

"Can't tell you. That would ruin the whole thing."

"What whole thing?"

"Shut up and suck my nipples till I cum."

My conscience held me back for a brief moment, but then I relented. It's not like she was giving me any real choice. "Okay," I mumbled with a mouth full of roasted breast. As long as I knew Little Mickey was okay, I could relax and enjoy myself. But then he stopped barking.

"Hey, is he okay?" I asked after like my fourteenth orgasm. She really brought it out in me. Or out of me, anyway.

"Sure. He was just picked up."

"Picked up? By who?"

"None of your business. Shut up and eat my pussy." Then she sat on my face, literally muffling my protests.

When she got off, so to speak, I spit feminine fluids and pubic hair from my mouth and demanded to be untied. She just laughed and laughed.

I heard a car driving away, and realized that must be Little Mickey. I mean in the passenger seat or trunk. Or maybe even at the wheel. Who knew anymore? We were all definitely living in the Era of Anything Goes. Logic had been reduced to a relic since nobody used it anymore, like telephone booths or 8-track tapes.

"Why did you bring me here if you weren't going to return my dog!" I demanded.

"You're such an idiot," she said, getting up from the bed. "But a good lay. That's really the reason I brought you here. Well, one of them. But your services are no longer required. We can take it from here."

"Who is 'we'? You and the voices inside your fucked-up head?"

"You're the one in restraints, by request. And I'm the crazy one?"

"Can one of you at least untie me?"

She didn't answer. I heard the shower. Then she came back in and got dressed, ignoring me. God, she had a great body. And my stuff was all up inside of it. Despite my predicament, I felt distracted by a sense of conquest. That's when I smelled the smoke. She had set the house on fire. Then she left me there, laughing as she left.

The flames began engulfing the living room, heading for the kitchen. If she had a gas stove, my goose was cooked. Worse. More like my bacon was burnt to a crisp, Elvis-style. I hated heat anyway, which is why I was living in Seattle, and the fumes from the fire was already choking my lungs. I finally passed out.

I didn't even fight it. Oddly, I felt ready to go. "Smoke Gets In Your Eyes" by the Mallet Men played in my head as everything faded to black.

When I opened my eyes, I was in another bed, and Laura was looking down at me. Yes, *that* Laura. The bartender from Navy Strength. My old flame, suddenly rekindled. She was delicately stroking my hair. A cool, wet cloth was draped across my sweaty forehead. I looked around and recognized her small but plushly appointed two bedroom apartment over in West Seattle, near our favorite date spot, West 5 Restaurant and Lounge. She had a roommate I'd never met. Maybe it was her other personality.

"I must be in heaven," I said. "And you're my guardian angel."

"Neither," she said. "Well, maybe the second one."

"How did I even get here?"

"I saved you from the fire. You were totally passed out. Good thing I showed up when I did."

"Well, gee, that was nice of you. It's good to see you again, too. Even under these rather bizarre circumstances. I missed you."

"Well, I wasn't planning on this reunion, but I guess it's good it happened, at least for the sake of my own conscience. And your life, of course."

"Um, okay. I'm a little confused. Maybe my brain is still hazy from the shock and the smoke."

"I just feel guilty for getting you into this mess. Are you feeling okay?"

"What mess? *This* mess? What do you mean, how are *you* involved?"

She looked at me for a pensive beat, then said, "I set you up, Vic. Remember? I'm the one who told you to place an ad for dog walking, but only so my mom could answer it."

"Your *what*?"

"Yeah, she's my mom, sort of. Dianne. I guess I should've told you that sooner. I had no idea what she was up to, though. You have to believe me, Vic."

"Why?"

"Because it's true."

"Truth is relative nowadays."

"True."

"I don't believe you."

"Doesn't make it any less true. She saw you at the bar one day, and told me to start sleeping with you so she could get close to you. Like a sex spy, sort of."

"Jesus." Then something else sharply hit me square in the brain. "So you carried me out of that burning house, all by yourself?"

"No. I was with someone."

"Who?"

"None of your business."

I sighed. "Nothing is anymore, apparently." God, she was cute. "Hard to believe any of this. You don't look anything like Dianne, for one thing."

"It's by marriage. Have you been listening to me, Vic?"

"Yeah, sort of. I'm having trouble following you, though. But then I'm a lousy detective."

"*Listen.*" She rather harshly smacked my face and resumed her spiel. "I'm trying to come clean here. My conscience wouldn't let me go on. That's why I quit the bar and stopped seeing you. I actually liked you, Vic. But I only started seeing you as a favor to my mom. Well, *step*mom. If I hadn't stopped by her house, you'd be dead by now."

"Why did you stop by her house?"

"I was tipped off."

"By who?"

"Friends on the inside, working undercover."

"Inside of what?"

"Some kind of syndicate trafficking in animals, or something. They're based in Costa Rica. My father is the CEO of a company with a branch down there, and somehow he's involved with this racket. Anyway, he's the one who really set all this up. I just went along, until I understood what was happening. I just like to make my father happy so he stays the fuck out of my life, but keeps paying my rent."

"You two are not close, I take it."

"Not at all. Geographically or emotionally."

"And your stepmother?"

"I hate her, too."

"Okay, then. Just another unhappy family, I get it. But you're on speaking terms, obviously."

"Just enough to keep the checks coming."

"I see. So are they holding the dog for ransom from Mickey Rourke or something?"

"I have no idea. Dianne is just doing what David told her to do, and I did what she asked me to do, before I realized what it was all about."

"Which is what?"

"I'm not sure. But it's not good."

"Not for me or the dog, anyway. Wait, so Dianne was married to your real father?"

"She still is."

"I thought she was divorced?"

"No, she's a widow twice over. She probably lied to you. She lies a lot. Lying is very fashionable these days, because it's been normalized in the mainstream. There's no need for 'fiction' anymore. Everyone just makes everything up anyway, to suit their own agenda. And then it's accepted as fact by people that choose to believe it."

"Skip the editorial."

"The fact is, her first husband died. In a fire. Peronally, I think she killed him. But I wasn't there to rescue him. I wasn't even born yet. Then the other one had a heart attack while she was on top of him, you know, having sex. I have my suspicions about that as well."

"Holy shit." I sat up, felt dizzy, then settled back down. I was dehydrated. Too much booze and smoke fumes can do that to you. It was a combustible combination.

Laura brought me some water and even held my head as I drank from the glass.

"So your last name is Thornton?" I asked.

She looked exasperated. "Jesus, Vic, you never even knew my last name! It's Palmer!"

"Huh? Your name is Laura Fucking Palmer?"

"No middle name, just Laura Palmer. After my real father, David Palmer."

"Wow. I had no idea."

"I told you that. More than once."

"You did? Wow. That's so freaky. Yet so cool. You look like Sherilyn Fenn, at least to me, and your name is Laura Palmer. No wonder I fell in love…" I stopped short, but it was too late. The cat was out of the bag, but still in the river.

"Let's not get carried away, Vic. For one thing, I don't look anything like Sherilyn Fenn. You're living in a fantasy world of your own making."

"Aren't we all?"

"Not nearly as much as you."

"Maybe Life is just a dream, and you're all simply phantoms that inhabit my consciousness, of my own subconscious design, and only *I'm* real?"

"That theory is a tad self-aggrandizing, don't you think?"

"Hey, nobody knows what the hell is going on, so all theories are on the table. But you look more like Sherilyn Fenn than your own mother, or stepmother, that's for sure.

But that's because she looks like Dyanne Thorne."

"Who?"

"*You* know, she was in the 'Ilsa' movies. 'She Wolf of the SS,' 'Harem Keeper of the Oil Barons,' 'The Wicked Warden,' 'The Tigress of Siberia'…"

"I'm afraid once again your references escape me, Grandpa."

"More evidence you're just a character in my dream."

"Maybe you're a character in mine?"

"No, I don't think so. Then why would you be fucking someone like me in your own fantasy?"

"That's my point. Look, Vic, I enjoyed our time together, but you're older than my father. And you fucked my stepmother. *After* you fucked me."

"Aw, shit. Don't tell me that." I felt like I was re-living *The Graduate.*

"But it's true. Not fake news."

"So you only went out with me as part of this whole elaborate scheme to kidnap Mickey Rourke's dog?"

"Yes. But now I'm going to help you get him back. Or at least point you in the right direction."

That's when I noticed Dianne's poodle was sitting on the chair across from us, eavesdropping. "Hey, that's Dianne's dog! I mean your Mom's! *Step*mom's!"

She picked up the poodle and held her. "No, Vic. She's mine. Well, my roommate's. My mom was just using her as part of the ploy."

"You mean *step*mom."

"You still had sex with a mother and her daughter, Vic."

"But you're not even related."

"Still. Pretty creepy."

"Hey, I didn't know! But *you* did!"

"Yeah. I'm messed up. I admit it, Vic. I'm sorry. But now I want to make amends. Here."

She got up and wrote down something on a sheet of

paper, and handed it to me. It said, "The Shameful Tiki Room." There was certainly enough shame to go around.

"Where's that?" I asked.

"Vancouver. Go here and ask for a bartender named Gary. He's my ex-lover. He will tell you where to find the dog."

"How would he know?"

"Well, he's also my brother."

"What?"

"*Step*brother. He's Dianne's natural son. By birth. So we're not related."

"And he was your boyfriend?"

"For a little while. More like a fuck buddy. We never actually lived together in the same house, so it's not like we were actually siblings. It's complicated."

"*I'll* say. You're chastising me for fucking your mom—*step*mom—and yet you fucked your own brother!"

"*Step*brother. And you fucked his *real* mother. I wouldn't mention that to him, though. You're probably going to have to beat any information out him, anyway."

She then handed me a picture of him that made me wish I still had a gun.

I shook my head in bemused disgust. "If there is a God, and He's watching, He must be laughing."

"*She*," Laura said. "And She's crying."

"Even if God is a babe, She certainly has a hard-on for yours truly. It would make sense if God is transgender, anyway. I mean, as much sense as anything."

"I wouldn't take the world so personally, Vic. It really doesn't care about you. It doesn't even know you exist."

"I almost didn't, not anymore, thanks to your *step*mother."

"Well, yeah, *that* I would definitely take personally."

"I do. Trust me."

She teared up suddenly, hugged me, and said, "Sometimes I wish *you* were my dad. Then life would be so much simpler."

I grimaced.

"Except for the sex part," she quickly added.

It didn't even bother me I'd been banging Dianne's stepdaughter. Donald Trump was president. The whole concept of right and wrong had been destroyed. It was always a fine line anyway.

After we made love for therapeutic reasons, Laura and I grabbed a quick bite at West 5, then went down to Alki Beach to watch the sunset as we made out. Afterward, she drove me back to my Corvair, still safely parked on the street in Wedgwood. Her mother's house hadn't totally burned down, but it had been badly damaged. Fire trucks probably arrived right after Laura and her mystery date rescued my smoldering ass.

"She's probably down in San Jose by now," Laura said. "This place was just a write-off, anyway."

"So she's in California?"

"No, the one in Costa Rica."

"I thought she had a place in Cabo San Lucas?"

Laura shrugged. "Maybe. I only know about the one in Costa Rica. She lives there with my dad most of the time."

"Jesus, why can't anyone shoot straight anymore?"

She looked at me with genuine concern and said, "I just hope you still can."

"Like Billy Idol sang, 'I don't need a gun'."

"Who?"

I kissed her goodbye. Then I drove home to my place in Ballard to pack up for my trip, but only after a nightcap at one of my favorite bars, Hazlewood. Then a quickie Mai Tai just down Market Street at The Albatross, a tiki-type joint. But then that was it. Promise. I mean, for the night.

I knew I couldn't go on like this. Eventually my liver would give out. I needed something to live for, though.

The truth, or part of it, is that I really didn't want to go rescue this dog. It felt like yet another misadventure had been thrust upon me against my will, and I wasn't even actively pursuing a dangerous course anymore. Far from it. I just wanted to be left alone in peace. Forever. But my conscience wouldn't allow me to just let this go. I had to save Little Mickey. Eventually.

However, being a Seattleite now, I was in no hurry to get started on this rudely imposed "case." I had become passive via ambient osmosis. As my favorite bartender at Hazlewood once observed in a casual conversation about Seattle's tentative traffic, "People here have no sense of urgency." It was true. Everyone was far too polite, at least by my native Brooklyn standards. There was no such thing as "road rage" around here. People in Seattle drive like they're in a funeral procession, or they're two-time losers afraid to get pulled over for the slightest infraction. Simply getting across town is like slowly racing through an obstacle course. Maybe as a younger man it would've bothered me a lot more. Now I blended right in.

When I finally stumbled home to my little one-bedroom apartment right off Ballard Avenue, my cat Doc was impatiently waiting for me, pacing like a worried wife. Whenever I was away on brief trips, the landlady looked after him for me. And no, I'm not banging her; she's like eighty years old, plus she's a lesbian, I think.

Also waiting for me was Ivar, the mysterious, vintage sailor statue that had been following me around since I arrived in Seattle two years prior. I still had no idea where he came from. He was about two feet tall, but loomed much larger in my psyche. Some nights I could swear I heard him clomping around the hardwood floor on his peg leg. He wouldn't stop smiling at me, either, like he knew something I didn't. I kept him around as a reminder that supernatural elements were at work, even if I had no idea what or why. Somehow that feeling comforted me. It meant there was more to life than met the eye, and perhaps there was a reasonable explanation for all this madness, somewhere beyond this realm. Or maybe there wasn't, and Ivar was just another sign of its random meaninglessness, an enigma without a solution. Either way, I was afraid to get rid of him. Plus I'd tried, via shooting, stabbing, drowning, you name it. But apparently I was stuck with him. At least his upkeep was cheap. Cats were much higher maintenance. So were women. Live ones, anyway.

I fed Doc and we snuggled up in my Murphy bed watching *Embodiment of Evil* starring Coffin Joe—which is in Portuguese, you know—until I fell into a deep sleep and dreamed about sex and death.

I might as well have still been awake.

Chapter Three
CANADIAN SUNSET-UP

The drive up I-5 to Vancouver was actually very relaxing, especially with my customized Mancini mix in the CD player. I'd only been over the northern border once before, just to check it out. Vancouver is a cool town with a beautiful natural backdrop, but I prefer Seattle. It has more grit 'n' grunge, so to speak, and therefore more character. Vancouver was too clean, almost to the point of being antiseptic. Still, I dug quaint little Gastown and scenic Granville Island and even The Lookout, their version of The Space Needle. This time I wasn't there as a tourist, which tends to distill one's perspective.

I was actually in pretty good spirits, all things considered. It was nice to have a good excuse to get out of town, as much as I loved my adopted home, and the cool breeze felt good in my clogged-up lungs, the pure Northwestern air ridding them of any lingering fumes. I kept coughing and was probably suffering from mild or maybe even semi-severe smoke inhalation, but I didn't go see a doctor, despite Laura's urging. I figured I'd met my medical quota for the decade already. As I told you earlier, my bout with Mickey Rourke had resulted in my first completely involuntary physical in years. I wasn't in the mood for yet another lecture on how I really needed to get a colonoscopy at my age. My ass was already sore enough from forced penetration. I didn't want anything else shoved up there just yet, metaphorically or otherwise.

Plus my diet was much healthier these days, at least per my unprofessional estimation. While daily flushing out my colon with fluids (okay, that includes booze, but that kills germs, right?), I'd also become a semi-vegetarian. I'd been thinking about this for years, due to my empathy for animals. And once I adopted Doc, that was it. Though I'd had pets, mostly cats, throughout my life, something about Doc—whom I suspected was imbued with the spirit of my late human friend—strengthened my resolve to get my protein from live pussy rather than dead meat. I did still eat eggs and seafood, though, which I guess makes me a pescatarian, technically speaking. Fish don't have any fur or feathers, just fins, and they don't answer to their name, so it was easier for my conscience to ignore their right to peacefully co-exist. Also, I could only eat so many beans before I started farting in bed, which would be fine unless I wasn't alone. And most of the time, I wasn't, by design. I cherish my isolation, but I dread true loneliness. I only hoped I wouldn't die alone, but I wasn't holding my breath in the meantime. That would be counter-productive. Plus once you're dead, you're alone, anyway. *Forever.*

I'd already decided on the three words I wanted on my tombstone: "That Was Weird." Though I planned to be cremated. Dianne almost beat me to it.

The casualties of my present state of peaceful resignation were hope for the future and nostalgia for the past. I mean, I still dug retro pop culture to an extent. But that was because I was too lazy and comfortably numb to broaden my cultural horizons. I still dressed like a Rat Pack reject, too, but mostly because I was too broke to update my wardrobe. Frankly, I just didn't get the same kick out of all that old stuff anymore, not like I once did. Maybe because I was old now, too. I felt an affinity for certain periods, aesthetically speaking, but didn't yearn to travel back there in a time machine or anything. The romantic glow of bygone eras had finally faded in my rearview mirror. I guess it was also because I had so much of my own past behind me now, and so little of my future in front of me. Things never seem more precious than when they're disappearing, whether it's bowling alleys, drive-ins, your reflection in the mirror, or the people and pets you love. It's hard to mourn things that are already gone when you're too busy trying to appreciate what's left.

Anyway, after I arrived in Vancouver, I checked into the same place I stayed in a year or so before during my first visit: a swanky midcentury modern-style motel called The Burrard, because it was on Burrard Street, smack in the middle of downtown, ensconced in gleaming, futuristic towers that made Vancouver's skyline look like a cosmopolitan Utopia, or Dystopia, depending on one's tastes in architecture.

After I dropped off my stuff I headed back out, drank a Manhattan or two at one of my favorite local bars, Prohibition in the Hotel Georgia, along with some kind of food, then I drove across False Creek to my actual destination.

It was dusk, the sky all pink and purple, as I pulled up to The Shameful Tiki Room on Main Street. I pretty much gave away what happened next with that cheesy chapter title, but then I've never been a big fan of mysteries anyway, even though I'm an ersatz "detective" who got his basic training via watching *film noir* rather than any type of formal education at a crime-fighting academy. To me, it's never the story itself that matters, but how it's conveyed. Every story has been told millions of times over thousands of years, in countless ways. What really makes a story special is the way one tells it, because no person experiences anything exactly the same, even if the experience itself is universal.

When I walked inside, "Twin Peaks Twist" by Messer Chups was playing on the sound system. *Again.* The very first time I'd heard this tune was way back at Navy Strength, the night I met Laura. Then I heard it again just recently in the Shanghai Room, when Dianne showed up. Now I heard it again as I saw Laura's stepbrother Gary, whom I recognized from the picture she showed me. Maybe it was just another cosmic coincidence, AKA Kismet, AKA Nobody Fucking Knows What the Fuck Is Going On So They Just Make Shit Up To Satisfy Themselves. Or maybe, as I often suspected, David Lynch was secretly directing my life, even picking songs for the soundtrack. No wonder neither Charlie nor Mickey could make good on their options. The movie of my life was already in progress, and I was the star without a script, just improvising.

Speaking of stars, I saw actors David Duchovny and Gillian Anderson huddled at a corner table. They were obviously taking a break from filming a new episode of *The X-Files*, yet another resurrection from the pop culture of my misbegotten youth. Either that, or they were exact lookalikes. Everyone, including me, pretended to ignore them anyway, just in case.

It reminded me of the time I was thrown out of a trendy Manhattan bar—frequented by celebrities treated by management like elite zoo animals, i.e. *look but don't approach*—for drunkenly telling Matthew Broderick that his remake of *Godzilla* sucked, but I still liked him. My date at the time has still never forgiven me. I learned my lesson. The hard way, as usual.

In appearance, Gary reminded me of Frank Stallone in *Barfly*, meaning big, muscular, and hairy, which didn't bode well for my well-being's immediate future, considering a testy confrontation was likely, given my touchy agenda. I decided to ease my way into an inevitably sticky situation, like using a cobweb as a hammock.

I sat down at the bar and nodded at Gary, who naturally didn't recognize me, or pretended not to, and ordered a Zombie, since there was a chance I'd be one of the undead before the night was over. In addition to the photo of Gary, Laura had given me a picture of Little Mickey that was actually taken while he was being surveilled during one of our walks together, I supposed by Dianne or one of her associates, so I was in the photo, too. I took it out and laid it on the bar next to a ten spot, which wasn't even enough to cover the drink.

"Is that my tip?" Gary asked dryly as he set my drink down.

"You mean this or that?" I said, nodding at both the photo and the bill.

He just stared at me without blinking or speaking.

"You're shy a few bucks for the drink," he said, setting a menu down in front of me for reference before he walked away without taking the money or even looking at the photo.

I reached back into my wallet and replaced the ten with a twenty, but set the photo on top of it. He took his sweet time getting back to me, and it wasn't even that busy.

Finally, Gary picked up the twenty. Then he noticed the photo and was about to set it back down when he happened to look at it.

"What's this?" he asked me without changing his facial expression.

"A dog."

"I see two dogs."

"Ha, ha. You recognize it?"

"Yeah, the one holding the leash is sitting right in front of me."

"How about the other one?"

Gary looked closer. "No. Why? Is it missing?"

"Matter of fact, yeah."

"So post some reward posters. I can't help you, man. This is a bar, not the fucking pound."

"Take another look. You've really never seen that dog?"

Gary looked again. "I don't know. They all look alike. I mean, it's a dog. A little dog. I've seen a million of 'em."

"Remind you of any in particular? Maybe one your

mother or stepsister might know?"

Gary stared at me a beat with those dead eyes. "So you're the guy."

"What guy?"

"The guy Laura said was coming up."

"You're just figuring that out?"

"I was trying to be polite."

"You mean evasive."

"You don't want to get involved."

"Involved in what?"

"The family business."

"Look, Fredo, I don't want to be involved more than necessary, either. I just need to find this dog."

Gary looked away, then back at me. "Okay, maybe I have an idea where it might be, but no promises. Out back. I got a five minute break due. Let's go."

I gulped down my Zombie, which probably explains my *chutzpah* regarding the inevitable, impending violence. We headed through the rear exit and into a dark alley. Gary got right to the point. He hit me once in the right eye. I could feel it swelling. I hit him back in the nose. It bled a little. Then we just stared at each other.

Finally, he said, "Just forget all this. Trust me. You don't want any part of this."

"I can't."

"Why not?'

"I have nothing better to do."

"Then you got too much time on your hands."

"But time just slips right through my fingers."

"Try replacing it with your dick. Oh wait, that would slip right through your fingers, too."

"That's not what your sister would say."

Then he hit me again, right in the mouth. Now it was really on. I'd have to defend myself with my fists. I no longer carried a gun for various reasons, the main one being I didn't think I needed one since retiring from the private investigation racket. Except I kept not retiring, and kept finding myself in predicaments where a gat would come in handy. To quote Clarence Worley i.e. Christian Slater i.e. Quentin Tarantino in *True Romance*: "It's better to have a gun and not need it than to need a gun and not have it."

I swung back and connected with his jaw. He barely budged, then socked me right in the nose. I felt blood spurt out, then swung back wildly, missing him. He gave me a quick, sharp jab in the gut, then another below my chin, and I was on my back. Shaking off the pain and dizziness, I picked up a beer bottle on the ground near me, stood up shakily, then smashed it across his left temple. He shook it off and wiped the blood from his face, then was about to hit me again when I punched him hard in the forehead. He teetered back, then I kicked him swiftly in the nuts. He bent over in agony, all the way down to his knees, cradling his crotch. Taking advantage of his vulnerability, I kicked him again in the face. This time he went down, lying on his back.

Fighting is a lot like fucking. The less you care about getting hurt, the better you get at it.

"Sorry," I said. "I meant *step*sister."

He sat up groggily, wiped his face, and said, "You fucked my mother too, didn't you?"

"Yeah. How did you know?"

"She told me."

"Well, damn. I can't deny it. I banged your mother *and* your stepsister. Not at the same time, though. Sorry. Nothing personal."

"I'm going to kill you."

"Is that legal in Canada? I mean homicide."

"They'd consider it a mercy killing. Like putting down a dog."

"How are you mixed up in this, anyway?"

"Like I said. Family business. Which means none of yours. And keep Laura out of it."

"Hey, she sent me here, slick. Not my idea."

"She doesn't know I'm working with my mother. They don't get along."

"But you and Laura do."

"We did."

"She told me you got along *really* well."

"Yeah, we had an affair. So what? Not blood related."

"Like you said. None of my business."

"Nope. Neither is the dog. Just forget about it."

"Laura wants it saved."

"None of her business, either. Just go home, slick."

"Thing is, the dog is really *my* responsibility. His actual owner will kill me if I lose his dog. I mean, like, literally *kill* me."

"Well, I'll kill you if you don't back off."

I sighed. "I've tangled with Mickey Rourke, and I've tangled with you. This turned out better, at least for me. So I'll take my chances. If you can't help me find that dog, I'll just find it on my own. I'm a detective."

He laughed. "You're a fucking dog walker."

"Which means I need my legs intact for the sake of my vocation, so I have to find that dog." It was indeed a unique synthesis of my talents, such as they were.

"You never will. Give it up. Too late."

"Why, is it dead?"

"Might as well be."

"What's the big deal about this one god damn dog, anyway?"

"You'll never know."

"I'll just go ask David Palmer, then."

"My stepdad? He won't help either. Plus he won't be around much longer himself."

"I see. He's going to meet the same fate as your mom's two previous husbands. One of whom was your actual father, I take it."

"My father died of a heart attack."

"Yeah, right. And David Palmer is going to die of so-called natural causes soon, too. Which would make your mother a wealthy widow. I mean wealthi*er*. Which kicks down to you as well, no doubt."

Gary didn't say anything, but he didn't have to.

"Dog food for thought," I said. "A tasty treat, anyway. You helped me more than you know. Thanks."

I just left him there, then walked back inside and through the bar to the front entrance.

On the way out, Duchovny—or his doppelgänger—looked right at me and said, "The truth is out there." Then he winked.

"You're telling me," I replied, shooting him with my forefinger. I whistled *The X-Files* theme as I walked out the door. Someone behind me laughed. But I was used to that.

As soon as I felt the rain on my kisser, I suddenly threw up my Zombie, a delayed reaction to that gut punch from Gary. Then immediately after this, while I was still stooped over the sidewalk, someone hit me with a hard object on the back of the head. Everything quickly faded to black as my face landed in a pool of my own vomit on the rain-slick sidewalk.

I woke up in a part of town that was not familiar to me. It looked industrial. I looked around. I was lying in the middle of a vacant lot, mostly fenced in, obviously marked for construction. I could see the Vancouver skyline in the distance, across the water, so I knew I was still in the same city.

Reflexively I checked for my wallet. It was still there. I looked inside. Nothing missing. I just had a headache. And no car, since my Corvair was still parked back on Main Street. I figured Gary had been the one who cold-cocked me from behind, just to get even. But then why drag me all the way out here?

It was dawn, but cloudy. I didn't know which direction to head. I just started walking and eventually saw a cab, snagged it, since I fortunately still had my wallet, and told him to take me back to the tiki bar, which was closed, but hopefully my Corvair was still parked across the street. It was.

However, there was a note on the windshield. It was wet due to the recent rain, but I was able to make out the few words scribbled on it: "*It's not Mickey's dog. It's worse than that. Danger, Will Robinson. Fuck off.*"

My initial impetus to retrieve the dog was so his owner, or the person I naturally assumed was his owner, wouldn't send me back to the hospital. But then I realized: No, that wasn't my only motivation. I really wanted to rescue the poor little pup, for his sake, not just mine. So that meant I wasn't fucking off any time soon. And I'd learned to ignore little notes left for me by strangers. They were nothing but roadmaps to places I didn't want to be.

I drove back to The Burrard, walked into my room, and discovered a beautiful naked Asian woman lying in my bed. Contrary to popular belief, this doesn't happen to me every day. Sometimes they're not Asian. Anyway, she was naked except for the gun she was holding, which was pointed right at my crotch. It was equipped with a silencer, meaning it was ready to fire without hesitation on short if any notice. Talk about sending mixed signals. My penis felt very conflicted. It only got half-hard in confused response.

I felt the bump on the back of my head. "Something tells me you're the one that hit me back at the tiki bar," I said.

"No," she said. "But I know who did. I knew you wouldn't take the hint, though."

"Who the hell are you, anyway? Not that I care, considering you're already naked in my bed and all, so we can dispense with formalities."

"I'm going to dissuade you from pursuing this case, one way or another."

"If you're giving me a choice between sex and violence, I always choose sex."

She put the gun back down on the bedside table. "I figured as much."

"Mind if I take a shower?"

"Only if I can join you."

"Oh, sure. Can I ask your name?"

"Yes."

"Your name is Yes? Like the band? As opposed to what, Doctor No?"

"You really are a smartass, Vic Valentine."

"So you know *my* name already."

"Of course."

"And yours?"

"You may call me Jade."

"I 'may' call you Jade. But is Jade your actual name?"

"Maybe."

"Jade what?"

"Just Jade."

"Oh, one of those."

"One of what?"

"One-name-wonders. Celebrities on a first-name-only basis with the whole planet. Prince. Sting. Madonna. Emmanuelle."

"Who?"

"You know, that character is all those erotic movies back in the Seventies. There were dozens if not hundreds of them, mostly rip-offs. Personally, I prefer the ones directed by Joe D'Amato."

I had her and I lost her. "You're dating yourself, Vic Valentine."

"Well, it's all I can afford. I'm a cheap date."

"You'll only have one name too if you don't heed my warning, and it will be 'Mud.'"

"Aw, fuck. Let's go take a shower so I can wash that shit off."

The sexy stranger soaped me down then blew me in the shower with a voraciousness that was almost scary. She actually bit my dick and drew blood, which she swallowed along with my semen. I responded by fucking her brains out back in the bed, both of us still soaking wet, filling her every orifice to overflow. I never used condoms in my life. I just didn't care about the consequences. When I was young, I chalked it up to naïveté. Also I was worried if I dawdled, my date would change her mind. Now I was just old, lazy, and cynical. Plus my sperm count was probably spent, anyway.

Fifteen or so minutes later, as we lay in each other's arms, panting and perspiring, I noticed the gun on the beside table. "Still plan on shooting me?"

"Depends," she said, kissing my chest.

"On what?"

"On whether you back off the dog hunt."

"Why do you care?"

"Let's say I have a vested interest."

"Wait. So you left that note on my car."

"Yes."

"So Little Mickey is not Mickey Rourke's dog."

"Not really. He was just taking care of it for a little while, for somebody else."

"How do you know?"

"I just do. It doesn't matter. You have no reason to keep looking for that dog. That's all that does matter."

"Are you working with Gary and Dianne?"

"Hell, no."

"But you want that dog for yourself."

"Yes."

"Why?

"None of your business."

I sighed. "Yeah, apparently there's a moratorium on my awareness of anything these days. But the point remains: that dog was put in my charge."

"Don't worry about it."

"Easy for you to say. You won't have your head twisted

by off by Marv in 'Sin City'."

"We'll get in touch with Rourke once we have the dog safe and sound. You'll be relinquished of all responsibility."

"So *you're* going to hold him for ransom?"

"No. But Rourke will never see the dog again. He'll be in good hands, though."

"Why should I trust you?"

"I have a gun."

"Okay, that works for now."

"And I paid you with my body."

"I admit that was like getting a raise. So to speak."

"Good. Go home."

"People keep telling me that."

"Then do it. Now."

"I can't. Sorry. My conscience won't let me. I need to find that dog personally and make sure he's okay. Otherwise I'll never forgive myself. At least not for this."

She sat straight up, her long, shimmering black hair clinging to her small, succulent, sweaty tits, her nipples poking in between strands like pink eyeballs. "So you let me fuck you for nothing?"

"Of course! I never turn down a free drink, or a free fuck."

"It wasn't meant to be *free*."

"Put it on my tab."

"You leave me no other alternative, then."

"You remind me of Lucy Liu," I said truthfully. She really did.

She rolled her eyes. "Fucking racist."

"How is that racist?"

"We all look alike to you, don't we?"

"You mean Asians or women?"

She closed her eyes as if thinking, "*I can't believe I just fucked this idiot.*"

Then she got up and gave me a good look at her tight, shapely ass. Some of my cum was dripping down her right

41

thigh. Life wasn't so bad for us white demons.

Except then she picked up the gun off the beside table and shot me in the thigh.

"*Fuck!*" I naturally exclaimed, gripping my leg.

As I lay bleeding and moaning, she calmly got dressed, put the gun back in her purse, kissed me goodbye on the forehead, and said, "Final warning."

I lay back in a puddle of my own blood and semen, wondering if other dog walkers had these problems.

Chapter Four
CANUCK ME

When I woke up around dawn I was still shot, unfortunately, and I hadn't moved. I'd tied a sheet around my upper thigh to stop the bleeding just before I passed out. It was only a flesh wound. Those still hurt.

As I lay there wondering what to do next, I reflected on the dreams I actually dreamt during my delirium, though they were typical of all of my nocturnal wanderings across time and space. In the dreams, I was much younger and obsessed with a beautiful female stranger, an angel that would make all my dreams come true and solve all my problems. The sensations, the euphoria, the emotions all felt painfully palpable, like they did when I was actually experiencing them, decades ago.

I fell hopelessly in love with various members of the opposite sex as a matter of routine, starting around age six and continuing up until I was in my forties, when I finally decided satiating my ravenous lust for the erotic if ephemeral feminine form was much more rewarding, at least in the short term, than the vain pursuit of eternal, romantic bliss, which was only a mirage. At least you can taste and touch a pair of tits, however fleeting the immediate gratification of these base instincts may be. Matters of the heart are much more elusive and abstract.

But throughout my midlife-crisis-driven, beaver-or-bust lechery, somehow those dormant romantic feelings remained locked inside me, like an imaginary memento from the murky past of a future that never was. And as my body rapidly aged and fell apart on me, I could feel the limitations of fleshly desires closing in on me like a fishnet. Fishnet stockings, anyway. Ultimately, vice created its own vise.

One reason I had counted on tracking down my soul mate was because my childhood was so lousy. My father was a crooked cop eventually gunned down by his drug-addled lover, who happened to be my high school sweetheart. My mother died in an insane asylum. My older brother jumped off a bridge when he was still a teenager. Only finding my True Love could rescue me from a similar fate, I wrongly reasoned. I embarked on that search with a resolute, passionate spirit that now only exists as an internally entombed ghost, emerging during my unconscious inner sojourns to taunt and haunt me.

For a long time I thought Rose, the main reason I became a quasi-private eye, was my personal savior. She wasn't. As it turned out, nobody was. Nobody should be. That's too much responsibility to lay on someone else.

But the bottom line was this: I was in my fifties and still alone, lying in a Vancouver hotel room, slowly bleeding to death, inside and out.

You may be wondering why I seemed so passive during two very close brushes with death within such a short time span. Of course, the sex before each took off the edge. You may also be questioning why all of these gorgeous women were so willing to instantly fall into bed with a broken down old geezer like me. I'm with you. I couldn't figure it out either. But I wasn't even trying. I think that may be a crucial part of the elusive explanation.

Anyway, I finally decided to give living at least one more chance to prove itself worthwhile. Instead of 911, I called Monica down in Portland. She was much more responsive and reliable than some stranger on the phone.

I explained my current circumstances. She didn't sound surprised.

"Vic, how long can you keep this up?"

"My dick? I don't know, frankly. It's getting tired."

"I mean all of it. I thought you were just a dog walker now?"

"I am! I mean, basically. I aspire to be, anyway."

"So why are you lying in a motel with a gunshot wound? Is that considered a standard job hazard in your new profession?"

"Well, I'm still relatively new at this. I deserve a learning curve."

"Jesus, Vic. I thought I could stop worrying about you and just enjoy my life."

"I thought you *were* enjoying your life these days, especially without me in it on a daily basis, bogging you down with my bullshit. How's your girlfriend, by the way?"

"She's great. She's lying right here next to me. We just woke up."

Despite my condition, my penis grew hard. I couldn't help it. It was a reflexive response to anything remotely erotic.

Monica might as well have been sitting right there beside me. "Take your hand off your cock, Vic."

I did. "You know me too well, Monica. I wish we'd gotten married."

A pause, then she said, "You never asked."

"I was dumb, what can I say. You're my best friend now that Doc is gone. You always were, in fact. And it's always a good idea to marry one's best friend."

"I love you too, Vic. But like a brother."

"One that you occasionally screw?" Monica and I had been fuck buddies for a long time, up until a few years ago.

"That's disgusting."

"But more common than you'd think."

"Huh?"

"Never mind." I tried sitting up, then groaned in agony. The bed was a gory mess. I'd have to leave the maid an extra generous tip. Maybe she'd take it out in trade. My cum rate was much more fluid than my cash flow.

"Vic, get yourself to a doctor. *Now*. You still have health insurance, right?"

"I don't know. Did Congress repeal Obamacare yet? I've been too busy to pay attention lately. Of course I'm in Canada now, so it doesn't matter, anyway."

"Vic. *Please.* Get yourself fixed up, forget this mess, and go home. And stop sleeping around so much. You're getting too old for that shit, as the saying goes. Find a nice, mature woman and settle down already."

"Well, if you're okay with a threesome…"

"Vic, you had your chance. I outgrew my crush on you a long time ago."

"So you're full lesbian now?"

"I love Maria, regardless of her sex."

My penis was still hard. "I better go now."

"Yes. To the hospital."

"I will."

"Promise me you'll take care of yourself."

"I do. I mean I will. As soon as I get off. The phone, that is. Thanks, Monica. I love you. Like a sister. I mean like a really hot stepsister. Or a cousin down South."

She kissed the phone and hung up. I finished myself off, adding more bodily fluids to the soaked sheets, then hobbled to the bathroom to clean myself up.

I got dressed in my usual shiny if rumpled sharkskin suit and skinny tie, though since I lost my Fedora I stopped wearing any kind of hat a while ago. I still had a full head of hair and I was at the age where I needed to show that shit off. I considered it one of my few appealing attributes, probably the reason so many young chicks wanted to fuck me: they had something firm to cling to while my weary face was groveling with worshipful gratitude between their fleshy young thighs.

After I checked out of the local clinic, I took a cab over to Gastown, leaving the Corvair back at The Burrard since

Jade had shot me in my right thigh, which was my main driving leg. The doctor had told me to stay off of it for a while, anyway, indefinitely delaying my return to Seattle. The nurse told me she'd be happy to further tend to my wound when she got off work.

The nurse's name was Fifi. Or so she told me. All of these dames were probably giving me fake names so I wouldn't try looking them up in the phonebook after they were done with me. Fine with me.

She was French-Canadian and in her forties, I reckoned, with bleached blonde hair, big blue eyes, juicy red lips, and large, bouncy tits that looked and probably tasted like two giant scoops of French vanilla ice cream. She also wore tons of makeup, especially thick on the mascara and blue eyeshadow, but that didn't bother me a bit. She also bathed in quality perfume, apparently, adding to her earthy allure. Plus I always had a thing for nurses, ever since Flora way, way back at the San Francisco blood bank, AKA "The Date That Never Was." That's another long, sad love story in a series of long, sad love stories.

I'm an unapologetic sex addict. Obviously. And an alcoholic, of course, though I'm still not sure I meet the technical definition, since I did quit drinking for a while, or at least cut back a bit. In any case, I tried going to AA and SLAA (the equivalent for sex and love addicts, like me) programs to cure myself, but I only wound up meeting other hopeless, horny drunks and fucking *them*. Which is why I still attended meetings sometimes. I guess I hadn't yet admitted I was powerless over my addictions. I also didn't give a shit anymore, as I keep insisting. I didn't want power over my passions. I wanted them to control me. I encouraged them. And look where it got me: Laid. Limping, but laid. My misery craved company, but only long enough to get my rocks off. Then I wanted my solitude back, largely so I didn't have to buy anyone else a drink.

I met Fifi at a cozy, popular Irish pub/restaurant on

Carrall Street in Gastown called Shebeen. The cobblestone streets and vintage lampposts of this neighborhood sort of reminded me of Philadelphia. But then Jade reminded me of Lucy Liu and Laura reminded of Sherilyn Fenn, so my references may be less than reliable. I still stand by them, if only out of stubbornness.

Fifi—who reminded me of Dolly Parton, except for her accent—and I small talked a bit as we drank our cocktails. I was drunk by my third Old Fashioned so I had trouble concentrating on her voice, only her luscious lips and mesmerizing cleavage. She went on and on about the medical profession and how superior the Canadian healthcare system was to ours. I agreed. Then we talked politics a bit, trashing Trump, though in truth, I've always been pretty apolitical. I never even voted. But I always hated that candy-colored clown anyway, long before his latest trashy reality show. I couldn't wait till it got cancelled. Not that I watched it, anyway.

Then we started talking about movies, a subject of actual interest to me, and naturally her tastes were way more mainstream than mine. Then we switched to music. I had to close this deal soon or else I'd lose interest. Fifi was one sexy NILF, but with extremely poor taste in pop culture.

None of that mattered when we were back in her nearby loft apartment on Abbott Street, fucking like the last bunnies on Earth. Fifi wasn't exactly my type intellectually, but she was a freak, which was just what the doctor ordered. The Lookout Tower gleamed outside her window with illuminated majesty, looming like an ominous beacon against the misty night sky,

She literally licked my leg wound and even squeezed it so she could suck out fresh blood. I thought maybe she was a vampire. At least I hoped so.

After she washed down some of my blood with some of my semen, I told her I had to get going.

She started crying so I hugged and kissed her and then

we fucked again and I left after she fell asleep. She was so lonely. My heart felt bad. But my leg felt much, much better.

Of course, it felt much worse after I walked out onto the wet sidewalk, leaned against the famous Steam Clock to catch my breath, then crossed Water Street and got slammed by a speeding car, sending me reeling over its windshield, roof and back onto the slick pavement.

It was very late, around two in the morning, so no pedestrians witnessed the hit-and-run. But Fifi, who had apparently heard the commotion, ran outside screaming, wearing only her bra and panties, and dragged me back up to her place around the corner. I hadn't noticed either the driver or even the make of the vehicle, much less the license plate, before it was gone.

She checked me out and found nothing broken, but I was pretty bruised and banged up and my leg was bleeding again. She licked my wounds, literally, until I got hard, then she sucked that dry, too. I passed out in her bed, wondering if that car had actually meant to kill me, or I just didn't see it coming.

But then I never do.

When I opened my eyes after recovering from yet another semi-traumatic injury, I heard Fifi talking on the phone in hushed tones in the living room. The conversation sounded like it was in French, I surmised, so I had no idea what she was saying, or to whom. And I didn't care.

With agonizing effort, I managed to put my clothes back on and went into the kitchen, hoping she would make us coffee, or at least some for me. She hung up the phone as soon as she saw me, which seemed a tad suspicious, but in my state I was understandably paranoid.

"I love hearing you talk in French," I said to her. "So sexy."

"That was Chinese," she said rather curtly. "Would you like some breakfast? I have to get to work. How are you feeling?"

Her bedside manner was much more business-like than it had been the night before.

"Okay, considering," I said. But I had to back this dialogue up a bit. "Wait, you were talking in Chinese just now? On the phone?"

"Yes. It's a common language around here. Vancouver is very cosmopolitan."

"But you're French," I said. I really was a moron, at least regarding linguistics and languages. All humans sounded alike to me. Something else I had in common with animals.

"So? I speak several languages. I've worked in hospitals all over the world. Now hurry up and decide. That's English, by the way."

"Damn. Okay. Can I just get some coffee?"

"Sure."

She turned on an espresso machine with all the enthusiasm of a vet giving a baboon an enema. I scanned her modest but comfy little pad. It was plushy appointed but extremely messy. She obviously didn't care much about appearances, except her own. Probably because she spent most of her time alone, without even a pet for company. I would've felt sorry for her, but I was too preoccupied with self-pity at the moment.

She gave me a quick kiss then rushed me out the door with the coffee still in my hand, telling me I could keep the cup, which I tossed in a trash can after I gulped it down. It occurred to me once I was back on Water Street that Jade was probably Chinese. The fact that a car ran me over and then I wound up staying with a French woman who spoke Chinese just seemed too bizarre to be a coincidence. But maybe it was. I was too weary to analyze it right then.

Man, I already missed being a dog walker, even though now I could barely walk anyone, including myself.

I took another cab over to Granville Island to grab some breakfast, ideally a crab omelette. I mulled over the possibility that I appealed to women's maternal instincts, even if they were my age or younger. That would make sense. I was like a stray puppy no one would adopt, only pet and feed then kick back out into the street. Again, I had no problems with that. I only needed temporary shelter. I liked being lost. It was my comfort zone.

I limped around the Public Market looking for a place to eat. There were too many options, but I was in no hurry. I felt weak, but not especially hungry. It was a breezy, cloudy day. The crisp, clean marine air felt good on my skin and in my lungs. It helped clear my head. The sounds of seagulls and seals was soothing to my soul.

The sudden sensation of a knife blade sticking sharply into my spine was not. Par for the course in this violent, pornographic cartoon called "My Life."

"Get in the car," an intimidating male voice said. I was relieved. My pecker needed a break.

As I obeyed orders and climbed into the passenger seat, I noticed the front fender of his bright, red 1960s Mustang was slightly bent, and the windshield was badly cracked. I couldn't believe he'd damage a classic car just for the sake of running me over. The door locked behind me, and then the driver came around and sat behind the wheel.

It was my new friend Gary.

I was about to greet him when he socked me in the kisser and told me to shut up, once again holding the blade to my throat. I complied.

He drove off the island and back toward The Shameful Tiki. We passed some of the many local sushi and dim sum restaurants, and my stomach started grumbling. "Can we at least stop and grab a bite?"

He socked me again, so I settled for the two knuckle sandwiches and kept my aching jaws shut for the duration of the ride.

It was then I noticed a silver car that looked like a bullet on wheels behind us. A couple of mean-looking guys poked their heads and arms and guns out and started shooting at us with what looked like Uzis, though I'm no arms expert. I do know a gun when it's being fired at me, though, and that's all I ever needed to know.

Gary cussed up a storm and sped up, but the back windshield had already burst and we both suffered minor cuts caused by the shattered glass. Then a bullet caught my shoulder, just grazing it but stinging like hell, and another blew out the back of Gary's skull, which made me actually appreciate my own wound.

The Mustang went careening off the street and crashed into a factory or warehouse or something. What a tragic waste, meaning the car. I managed to get out before it exploded, causing a massive fire. People were running and screaming, away from the inferno. I limped away just as the silver bullet car slowly drove by. I didn't think they saw me, but I couldn't be sure. Fortunately the sounds of wailing sirens as well as the chaotic destruction dissuaded any guilty bystanders from loitering around to finish the job.

Poor Gary's body was burning in the wreck, but hopefully he was already dead. It's all relative, after all.

Damn, that was a cool car. I mean it was bad enough he fucked it up running me over. But then to just explode in a ball of fire like that? Such a shame. Cool explosion, though. If it had to go, that was definitely the way.

I kept limping down a back alley and some desolate side streets until I came to a quiet, suburban neighborhood lined with the kind of hypnotically green trees you only see in the Pacific Northwest. It was so peaceful and quiet I nearly laughed. Or cried. I couldn't tell the difference anymore.

Trying to remain as inconspicuous as possible, I continued down the shady street until yet another sleek car pulled up beside me. It was a recent model Ford Thunderbird, ice blue in color, with tinted windows to block out the sun. The passenger window rolled down, and there was my other new friend Jade, holding her old friend, the silencer, aimed straight at my face.

"Just kill me already," I said wearily. "I'm fucking tired."

"Get in," she commanded.

Too weak to argue, I did as I was told. Plus her gams looked so incredible, stretched out between her black leather mini skirt and snakeskin pumps. She was wearing a leopard pattern blouse and no bra, because I could see her pointy little nipples.

My concentration on her ass was broken by the butt of her gun on my nose. "*Ow,*" I said. "Can you please stop being so mean to me? What the fuck? I'll leave town already. I don't care about the god damn dog anymore. I just want to get the fuck out of Dodge. Now. Alive." Which was a lie. I was very worried about Little Mickey. When I had a chance to be, anyway.

"Change of plans, Vic," Jade said. "Now I need you to help me find and then protect that dog. I'll pay you. In pussy."

I smiled and gently stroked her thigh.

She responded by hitting me in the nose with the gun butt again.

"*Fuck! Stop it!*" I cried.

"No time for that right now, Vic. I need you to concentrate."

"Then quit hitting me in the fucking head!"

"Sorry," she said insincerely. "But you only think about one thing. That's why I got it out of the way back at the motel."

"Are you kidding? That's not appeasement. It's encouragement. It's not like one fuck will fill me up. My tank has a leak, baby."

"Consider it an advance."

"How did you know I was such a sucker for sex?"

"Besides the fact you're male?"

"Yeah, besides that."

"Your reputation precedes you, Vic Valentine. Plus I've seen you at meetings."

"What meetings?"

"Sex and Love Addicts Anonymous. That's where Fifi saw you first, too. At a SLAA meeting in Seattle, months ago. We've been tracking you ever since. Don't ask me why, not right now. We need to move. Plane to catch."

I didn't even know where to begin responding to this barrage of information. But I already regretted ever attending those damned meetings. Or maybe I didn't. I was too confused.

"You're working with Fifi?"

"Yes. She was supposed to keep you safe in her apartment."

"She didn't exactly lock me in."

"I know. I think she set you up for Gary."

"So she betrayed you."

"Apparently she's working for the other side now. One of them, anyway."

"How many fucking sides are there?"

"Never mind. Stay on my side and you'll be fine. Just go along with me, whatever I do. Trust me."

"Why should I? You fucking *shot* me!"

"I thought it would slow you down, at least. Plus I was pissed you used me for sex. We had a deal."

"It was on the table, but okay, yeah. I never had any intention of giving up the canine quest. But now it's gonna be hard for me to walk dogs, with this limp."

"That was the idea."

"Well, that's my livelihood. So I have nothing to go home to, especially now."

"I thought you were a detective?"

"Not anymore."

"You carry a gun?"

"Not anymore."

"Well, I still need you. I thought the dog was here in Vancouver, but he's not. He's in Minneapolis. That's where we're headed now. I have your luggage in my trunk. The car will be delivered to your home down in Ballard."

"Don't you need the key?"

"Don't be naive."

"How do you know where I live?"

"I told you, Fifi and I have been following you."

I had no privacy anymore. Maybe I never did. You, either. "You're working with Dianne?" I asked.

"No. Gary and her want the dog for their own agenda. They'd prefer it dead than alive, after it's served its purpose. I'm just trying to save it. As well as the entire human race."

"Wow. Well, that's certainly a noble ambition, I guess."

We drove a bit, and then I had more questions. So many more.

"Why the tinted windows?"

"I'm sensitive to the sun."

"Me, too."

"I know."

"Did Dianne order Gary to kill me?"

"Yes."

"Why?"

"Because she thought you were working for her opposition."

"Why would she think that?"

"Because you were taking care of the dog. She figured you were part of the plot to keep him hidden."

"So who killed Gary?"

"Hal."

"The computer from '2001'?"

"What? No. You'll meet him soon enough. He knows where the dog is. Or so he tells me."

"Are you working with him?"

"Yes, and no."

"That's wasn't a multiple choice question, so it doesn't require a multiple choice answer."

"More will be revealed. For now, just keep your mouth shut and pretend you're my bodyguard."

"I'm the best you can do?"

"For the price I pay, yes. Plus you're available, and I'm in a hurry."

"So if this isn't Mickey Rourke's dog, whose is it?"

"A Russian."

"Where's he?"

"Russia."

"So are you returning the dog to him?"

"No."

"Then I guess I can't call him Little Mickey anymore. I guess I'll just name him...Fido."

"Gee, that's original."

"I mean after the zombie. You know. The Canadian zombie movie?"

"No"

"Well, it's one of my favorites. So Fido it is."

"It doesn't matter what you call him if we don't find him."

I sat back and relaxed as she drove to Vancouver International Airport. I fell asleep right away and dreamed of my long lost true love, who was faceless, but not titless. We were sitting by a lake having a picnic. Then one of Roger Corman's *Humanoids from the Deep* suddenly rose from the tranquil waters and amorously attacked her as I watched.

Next thing I knew Jade was smacking me in the face, trying to wake me up.

"What were you dreaming?" she asked me.

"Why?"

"You have a boner. And you're smiling."

I shrugged. "Just about the person I used to be, and the one I am now."

"And that's funny?"

"No. Sad. Very sad."

"Well, we're not dreaming anymore, Vic. Wake up. It's time to go." She dropped my passport on my lap. She'd thought of everything, with total access to my entire life, apparently. She was like a much sexier version of Google.

She parked in the long term lot and the next thing I knew we were on a plane for Minneapolis. I'd ever been there, or to its Twin City, St. Paul. The closest I'd been was Chicago, back in 2005. But that was another sad story of sordid sex and senseless tragedy. I hoped this one would be different. But probably not, given my track record.

I fell asleep almost immediately on the plane, even though normally I could never sleep on planes. My dream of long lost love resumed, but this time, it was much more innocent and pure, just like in my youthful, bygone days of optimism and hope.

I was in for one rude awakening.

Chapter Five
MINI-CRAPOLIS

Our rendezvous point was Psycho Suzi's Motor Lounge, the most elaborately decorated tiki lounge I've ever been to outside of the Mai Kai in Fort Lauderdale, Florida. I had not been expecting such a monument of Polynesian Pop smack in the middle of suburbia, smack in the middle of the country. For most people visiting the area, the Mary Tyler Moore statue and First Avenue nightclub downtown, Prince's music studio/mansion just outside city limits, and the Mall of America in nearby Bloomington were probably among the area's biggest tourist attractions. But me, I always made a beeline straight for the nearest bar with the best cocktails. Then it didn't matter where I was, because I felt right at home.

Psycho Suzi's comprised three separate, distinct stories of exotic kitsch, though the music didn't match the decor. They were playing classic rock. "Sweet Home Alabama" and "Werewolves of London" weren't exactly tiki music. But after I ordered my drink in a signature mug, I didn't care much about the ambient sound. I was just digging the scene.

Each level had its own name: Shrunken Head, Forbidden Cove, and Ports of Pleasure. We sat at the thatched bar in the Shrunken Head section, and indeed my drink was called a Shrunken Head. Sounded like my dick.

"So you make a living as a dog walker?" Jade asked me.

"I don't know if I'd call it a living. I'm augmenting a chunk of change I got when this piece of property in San

Francisco got sold. The owner left me a piece in his will. But it's running out fast."

"You should've invested."

"I don't know anything about finance."

"You're content being a broke bum?"

"Actually, yes, I am. Thanks for asking."

"Sad, really."

"Why, you think I'm wasting my potential?"

"For what?"

"Exactly."

"No plans for the future?'

"Just death, I guess. I feel dead inside already, anyway. So even that will be anti-climactic."

"You sound like one of your shares at SLAA."

"Are you a sex addict?"

"No. I can control it. I use it to barter."

"My kinda currency."

"Just remember to keep your mouth shut. Don't ask any questions. Hal doesn't suspect my true motives, so don't blow my cover."

"Are you fucking this guy Hal?"

"None of your business," we both said in unison.

She suddenly took out some bright red lipstick from her purse along with a little mirror, and applied it with delicate sensuality, puckering up in the process. "Men are so weak, sexually speaking," she said. "It's a genetic defect, I suppose. But one women can use to our advantage."

Before I could concur, our contact showed up. Hal Nickerson was a neatly coiffed, middle-aged gentleman, looking very sporty, dressed in a blue blazer and tan slacks. He had the air of an aging frat boy. Just too neat and clean. I immediately distrusted him. His perfect teeth seemed downright sinister, as if they'd been engineered by a scientist creating a master race of androids, disenfranchising the entire dental profession in the process. My teeth looked like a row of subway urinals by comparison.

Jade made the introductions. "Hal, this is Vic. He's the one."

"The one what?" I said, but nobody answered.

Hal smiled and shook my hand, but didn't respond directly to Jade's comment. "I've heard a lot about you, Vic. Going back a long, long time. Let's get a table, shall we? Drinks on me."

"Hell, yeah!" I said like the bottom-feeding bastard I was, disregarding his own mysterious comment. Jade rolled her eyes.

She kept ignoring me and I kept not caring as we sat next to each other across from Hal, who was still smiling like a sociopathic politician about to vote on a bill that would make the rich richer and the poor drop dead. But hey, he was paying, so that was fine with me, since I was a lifelong member of those legions of destitute deadbeats.

As soon as we were seated, a big, burly, muscular, bald, white dude in his thirties or so, with jailhouse tattoos all over his bulging biceps and thick neck, stood next to us, without sitting down or saying a word or even changing his facial expression.

"Shit," Jade whispered.

"Who's that?" I asked.

"His name is Brett Wheeler," Hal said. "He works for me in various capacities. Bouncer, bodyguard, collector, protector. Whatever I need. But don't mind him. He doesn't work unless and until he needs to. And I'm assuming he'll have the night off. Right, Jade?"

"Right," she said somberly.

Then Hal asked me, "Oh, Vic, I didn't have Brett frisk you, since I wanted to give you the benefit of the doubt as a diplomatic gesture of trust, but I assume you're not carrying a piece, right?"

I looked at Jade, then back at Hal, and shook my head. "Not any more. Too many mass shootings in the past few years. Bums me out. I lost my taste for firearms. Plus as a dog walker, I don't really need to be packing anything but poopy bags, dig?"

Hal laughed. "Good! Just checking. Anyway, we'll have a round here just to get acquainted—or in Jade's case, re-acquainted—then we'll talk terms for the dog's retrieval."

"What's wrong with this place?" Jade asked.

"Nothing. It's just a meet 'n' greet. First pleasure, then business."

"What exactly is the business?" I asked. "Dog food?"

Jade nudged me.

"Something like that," Hal said. "Let's all just relax for now."

That wasn't possible. The tension between Jade and Brett was palpable. They avoided any eye contact. They obviously had some personal history. I couldn't tell whether she felt intimidated or vulnerable or both. We all silently shared a Scorpion Bowl, then since Hal was on the hook, I ordered a Mai Tai to go. The waiter laughed, like I was joking, which I was, then he fulfilled my order in a blue mermaid mug.

"Okay, let's go," Hal said.

"I have to finish this."

"I thought you ordered it to go?"

"I did, but I was just kidding."

"Well, I'm not. Just take it. Trust me, no one will bother you. Not with me."

"Where are we going?" Jade asked.

"Another bar, not quite a tiki bar, but with a similar theme. You'll like it. Follow me. And drink up. I'm driving."

Then we all walked out as I sipped my Mai Tai out of my stolen mug, which I continued to imbibe on the ride over inside Hal's innocuous looking mini-van, the kind any soccer mom would own.

61

Except for the black-tinted, bullet-proof windows, of course.

Donny Dirk's Zombie Den on 2nd Street—now gone already, so don't look for it—was a lot smaller and even darker than Psycho Suzi's, and the music was much better. There were some stills from *Dawn of the Dead* (the original and only, in my book) on the wall, and Robert Drasnin's classic album *Voodoo* was playing on the sound system. Suddenly I felt better about life. But as usual, my sense of well-being was short-lived.

We hadn't been there five minutes when someone bit me on the shoulder while I was just standing around in the crowd, ostensibly in line for a drink. It was some stoned-out looking hippie freak. He nearly took a chunk of my flesh, but mainly just wound up with a mouthful of sharkskin. My jacket was ruined, especially when he drooled blood down the sleeve. *My* blood.

I screamed "*fuck!*" and looked into his eyes, which were bloodshot but vacant, his expression equally still, as if he were in a trance. His skin was pale, almost gray, and seemed to be decaying or something. His hair was long, stringy and dirty.

Before anyone around us had time to react, Brett grabbed the hippie cannibal freak by the arm and then lifted him over his shoulders and carried him outside through the back. Then I thought I heard a gunshot, but maybe I was just projecting my own hostility at the moment.

A minute or so later, Brett came back in, alone. By now we were huddled at a table in the corner. The place was dimly lit and crowded and the music was loud, so I guess that's why being attacked by a stoned-out hippie cannibal freak didn't cause more of a stir. Nobody likes a buzzkill.

Jade had grabbed some napkins to put on my wound.

"Who the fuck was that?" I asked. "Some junkie with the munchies?"

"He won't bother you again," Jade said, examining my wound with clinical detachment. "You're not bleeding anymore. It wasn't deep enough." She removed the blood-drenched napkins from my shoulder. My shirt was torn, and my stained jacket was lying across my lap. The bite hurt, though he'd barely broken the skin. It was just the whole idea of it that bothered me. No one else seemed to share my concern.

Hal showed up with a round of cocktails. I didn't even know what mine was, though I tasted bourbon, which meant it worked for me. I poured a bit on my shoulder wound, then downed the rest in a gulp. The gunshot in my thigh still hurt like a mother, too. Even my cheek where Jade smacked me still stung a bit. Not to mention my bullet-grazed shoulder from back in Vancouver. Both of my arms felt numb and limp. I'd have to learn to jerk off with my feet.

"You okay, Vic?" Hal asked.

"Not really," I said.

"Sorry about that," Hal said. "Any wooziness or anything? A cramping of the muscles? Maybe blurred vision?"

"What? No. I mean, I guess not. I just feel fucked up."

"Just drink, Vic. Best medicine there is. Kills everything."

I nodded and finished my drink, and he pushed over another one. Nobody else was drinking, though. All three cocktails were for me. But then I needed them the most, I figured.

"So where's the dog?" Jade asked Hal.

"Houston," Hal said.

"What?" Jade was pretty upset. "I thought you said you had him here?"

"No, I said I knew where he was. And that's Houston. At David's place."

"How do you know?" Jade asked.

"Because David told me."

"So why didn't we go directly there?"

"Because I needed you here first." Hal looked at Jade. Jade looked at Hal. They communicated something I couldn't see or hear. Jade grew eerily quiet.

"Why the hell is that dog causing such a fuss, anyway?" I demanded, slurring my words. "And why do you need me? I'm just a dog walker, for Chrissake."

"Because that dog holds the key to a cure," Hal said.

"Cure for what?"

"For the virus now coursing through your veins."

"What?" I spit out my drink. "You fucking *poisoned* me, asshole?"

Hal laughed. "No. That's just to make you feel better, at least for the moment. The virus was transmitted by the man who bit you. He's one of our early test subjects."

I tried to focus, but I was seeing double now. Double fucking trouble, that is. "For. *What*."

"We're calling it the Zombie Virus for now," Hal said. "You'll sleep well, Vic, in a comfortable bed. Next to Jade. Then tomorrow, all of your questions will be answered."

"Like what happens when we die?" That's when my head hit the table.

Chapter Six
EXPERIMENT IN ERROR

Instead of leaving for Houston first thing the next morning, Jade took me sight-seeing around town, to all those touristy places I mentioned earlier, just to kill time, which was better than killing me, I guess. Apparently Hal had to take care of some "urgent business" that suddenly came up. She was still very solemn, obviously hiding something, so I was hoping some time alone would result in more information, even though I was already suffering from a bad case of TMI. At the very least.

We stood together on Stone Arch Bridge, looking down at the Mississippi on a cool, breezy, overcast day, which made us feel a little better. We both hated the sun.

"I wish I could explain everything," she said.

"Why can't you?"

"It's complicated. Things are not what they seem. The process is already in motion, and there's nothing either of us can do about it."

"What the hell do you mean?"

"Last night was a controlled experiment. That freak was *supposed* to attack you. In fact, he was following orders, too. He just wasn't aware of it, since he was basically under hypnosis. But you aren't, not yet, anyway, which is interesting. This is why you're valuable to us, Vic."

"So that's why you brought me all the way here? Just so some hippie cannibal freak could chomp on me?"

"Yes. That way we, or at least Hal, could examine the effects of a human bite on another human, immediately after it happens."

"Get the fuck outta here. Seriously? I'm supposed to believe that."

"I'm a scientist, Vic. Fido is one of our test subjects. Now so are you."

"Test subject for what?"

"Fido was infected with a form of rabies, I guess you could call it, after eating a certain kind of dog food being produced in Costa Rica. It was originally made in Hong Kong. Out of dogs."

I sighed with terminal disgust, then verbalized the obvious, as is my wont. "So it really is a dog-eat-dog world.".

"It's much worse than that, Vic. Remember that case in Miami in twenty-twelve, when that naked guy attacked a homeless guy and started eating him?"

"Yeah! The start of the real zombie apocalypse! Or so I hoped. Then they blamed it on, what was it, bath salts?"

"Yes. But it wasn't bath salts."

"What was it?"

"Dog food. The kind Fido ate."

"Wait a minute. So you're saying you want to know if a human that eats that dog food will turn into a cannibal?"

"Not exactly. We want to know if a human bitten by a human infected with the virus will also become a cannibal. If it's a contagion, we have a problem. That's where you come in."

"I don't even eat animals."

"That's not part of the experiment."

"Wait just a fucking minute here, Jade. This has been your plan all along?"

"Not my original plan, but yes, I've been complicit in its implementation. Fifi and I were hired to keep tabs on you, and the SLAA meetings seemed like the easiest way, since you were there so often, cruising. We were still following you when Dianne tied you up in her house and set in on fire. That's when we called Laura to come get you. We didn't want to do it ourselves, and get made by Dianne or anyone working with her."

My head was spinning like a tiny tornado trapped in a toilet drain. "Who exactly is behind all this shit?"

"At the very top? An international conglomerate, cofounded by Hal Nickerson and David Palmer years ago, just after they both graduated from Stanford. Besides dog food, they're partners in a variety of businesses around the world, including pharmaceutical companies. I was working in one of their research labs. That's how I met David, then Hal. It's just part of my cover so I could infiltrate their ranks. Now I'm in so deep, I'm afraid I'm becoming more of an enabler than an enemy. I actually brought you to Hal, on his orders. I was hoping if I shot you, you'd be of no further use, or I'd scare you away for good. It didn't work. So here we are."

"So you didn't really bring me here to help you, but to help Hal."

"Well, you are helping me maintain my cover."

"You're going to owe me some serious pussy."

"Too late for that, too. You've been infected."

"So I can't even fuck anymore?"

"Not until we give you the right antidote."

"Great! The one thing I still in enjoy in life, you just took away."

"Only temporarily. Unless you have sex with someone already infected."

"That's only incentive for me to go bite someone."

"Please don't."

"I won't. Yet."

"Thank you."

"You are welcome. So Palmer isn't involved in this whole zombie scheme? Talk about voodoo economics."

"No, he only wants to make dog food out of dogs."

"Oh, that's all? What a cold-hearted prick."

"True, but Hal is the truly diabolical one. His plans are

much more ambitious, and potentially catastrophic."

"What the fuck does *that* mean?"

"Well, he's trying to prevent one outbreak, which he can't control, so he can subversively start another one, which he can control. Hal needs to contain this mutation of the virus, whatever it is, before it spreads any further. He's been experimenting with a way to taint mass market food with addictive mind-control drugs ever since he was a frat boy. He only co-founded the dog food company so he'd have access to a commercially produced product. But the main goal is to infect the human population by contaminating human food. Dogs were the first test subjects, then people. So far it's only resulted in cannibalistic freaks, in both dogs and humans."

"Speaking of dogs, this all sounds like a plot from 'Scooby Doo' that was rejected for being too unrealistic."

"Except this threat is all too real, Vic, as fantastical as it sounds. And the danger is urgent, even if it seems merely subversive for now."

"But that Miami incident was years ago. Why the concern now?"

"That was the only reported attack. There have been others all over the world. Russia. China. Asia. Europe. South America. Even Africa. Recently there's been a spike in incidents, all suppressed. If the virus takes over the population in its current state, it will be counterproductive, because the population will be beyond corporate or Government or even military control. The idea is subconscious manipulation, and this drug, derived from opioids, has the effect of subliminal hypnosis. At least until it was corrupted by unforeseen biological interference."

"I have no idea what you just said, which leads me back to the same question I keep asking, but which nobody will answer: why the fuck do you need me? I don't give a damn about the human race. Put it out of its misery, like a sick dog, and take me with it, for all I care."

"The virus is mutating very rapidly, Vic. Which means be careful what you wish for."

"You mean like death?"

"Yes. We're afraid it may now prove fatal. We needed someone expendable, to study up close, in order to counter its adverse, unplanned effects. Someone nobody would miss, but not just another homeless bum whose senses have rotted away. We needed someone sentient, that would actually understand what was happening to them, or at least be conscious of it, so they could give us intelligent feedback, on the spot, as the virus was eating away at them. Sorry, Vic. After much study, research, and surveillance, that person turned out to be you."

"I'm flattered, really. But so, like, if I haven't gotten sick yet, maybe then I'll be okay? And then you can just let me go home and everyone can go back to, like, doing normal stuff with their fucking lives?"

"Well, not yet. The test subject last night didn't really take a good bite out of you, so we will have to try again to make sure. I'm only here to observe and consult once the final results are in."

"Try *again*? What do you mean?"

Just then a big badass black dude with red eyes, wearing tattered clothes, drooling like a bloodhound, lunged at me from nowhere and bit me on the neck. "*Son of a bitch!*" I cried. I was going to yell "*fuck*" again but there were little kids around.

Then the giant zombie lunged at Jade, who quickly took out her silencer from her purse and shot the poor bastard in the forehead. He fell over the rail and into the river below. The few bystanders were too busy checking in on Facebook to notice, which was too bad for them, because this would've made one hell of a status update. Somehow spreading a "zombie virus" amongst the general population as it already existed seemed ridiculously redundant to me.

As I limped along, holding my neck with blood

trickling between my fingers, Jade just keep talking in a very calm voice, following close behind without touching me. "Brett was our first experiment with the new, improved strain of the virus," she continued, as if I really gave a shit at this point. "He's not violent, I mean no more so than usual, but he has become passive, like he's on antidepressants, which is a step in the right direction. He's now under Hal's complete control, like a true zombie, the old-fashioned kind, in voodoo lore, not the Zack Snyder movie kind."

"You mean the late George Romero," I said, bent over in agony. "He invented the fucking genre."

"I prefer the remake of 'Dawn of the Dead,'" she said.

"Really? I can't believe I slept with you."

She patted down my neck wound with a handkerchief, careful not to get any on herself.

"So will I be a fast zombie or a slow zombie?" I asked.

"At your age, probably slow."

"Good. I'm a purist." I couldn't tell if she was kidding or not. I couldn't tell if I was kidding or not, either. But she kept talking while I just sat on the ground, bleeding. Again, everyone on the bridge simply passed us by, totally oblivious, their gazes buried in their cell phones.

She knelt beside me and said, "I never thought my job would include kidnapping and murder. But I promise to get both of us out of this, somehow. Just trust me."

"I still don't understand how *I* got involved in all of this, of all the losers on Earth. I'm just a dog walker, for Chrissake."

"Full disclosure: you were marked the minute you started walking Mickey Rourke's dog. Because Fido was the first dog that didn't become a cannibal, or vicious, after digesting the corrected formula. However, he did bite someone that became infected, so that means the virus is still being transmitted in its detrimental form, at least to humans. The question now is, if a dog carrying the virus can infect a human, can an infected human infect another infected human?"

"Me."

"Yes."

"Well, what happened with the guy Fido bit?"

"He's been disposed of due to his dangerous behavior."

"Like the dude now floating down the river."

"Exactly. Beyond help and now only a danger to society. I am just trying to keep as many people safe as possible, given the conditions."

"How sweet. So, now what?"

"Well, we'll see. That one definitely looks like it broke the skin and got in your bloodstream. Now we just wait. Don't worry, I'm keeping a close watch on you, and I know what to do in case…anything happens."

"You mean shoot me in the head."

"Hopefully it won't come to that. The weakened version of the virus is obviously useless. We need to start all over. But first we need to fix the problem so we know how to prevent it from reoccurring in future formulas, by studying how it interacts with human physiology. Just hang in there with me, Vic. The researchers are at the top of their fields and they may find the antidote any minute. They're trying to derive it from the weaker strain of the virus, but so far, no luck. That's why we need to find Fido. His blood may contain the cure, since he's a carrier, but not a victim."

"Just shoot me now. Really. Like you said, I have nothing to live for. Especially now that I can't even fuck, my final pleasure."

"But you do have a reason to live, Vic. And I don't mean as a test subject. If you survive, I need you to help me defeat Hal from the inside."

"My incentive being? Now that sex is no longer an option?"

"Well, it will be if they cure you. I promise to make it up to you."

"And if not?"

"It won't matter."

"Because I'll be dead anyway. I don't suppose you're a necrophiliac, by any chance?"

She shook her head, then looked down in shame.

She helped me up and we walked slowly over the bridge and sat on a bench in the park on the other side a while. I didn't start frothing at the mouth or anything, though. Not yet, anyway. I thought of Marilyn Chambers in that David Cronenberg movie *Rabid*.

"You're really a scientist?" I asked.

"Yes."

"You don't look like any scientist I've ever met."

"How many scientists have you met?"

"I don't know. I thought you wanted to be an actress or model?"

"No, that was just to get me through school. That's such a shallow occupation. I didn't graduate from Harvard and Oxford just to pose for fashion photographers. I wanted to do something important with my life."

"And this is it?"

"I thought it was. Now I'm not so sure. If I can prevent a pandemic, and foil a plot to conquer the world, then I will feel useful."

"Are you sure you can't grant my last request and give me a blowjob? You can spit it out, that's okay."

"Not now that you've been bitten, so sorry. We're not sure if you can transmit the virus with semen, not just blood and saliva."

Without the prospect of sex, it hit me just how shallow and meaningless my life had become. I literally had nothing to look forward to now. I had some great memories of sex, which I could beat off to, but you can't even reminisce when you're dead. Now I just wanted to satisfy the one part of me that didn't pose a direct threat to anyone but myself: my nagging curiosity. "How and why did you get mixed up in this canine cannibalism racket?"

"I'm working for a secret organization."

"What's it called?"

"What part of 'secret' did you not get?"

"You must be The Girl from N.O.Y.B."

She considered that for a moment. "None Of Your Business."

"Yup."

"Okay, that works."

"Whatever. So how did Hal even think of this shit? Is he just a crazy fucker or what?"

"Insane, but brilliant."

"Being smart is not compensation for being sick. You could say the same thing about Manson or Hitler or Limbaugh."

"His present path started long ago, Vic. He was always innovative, but not always evil. This company in Hong Kong, co-founded by Hal and David, was the first one to try making dog food out of dogs. Nobody on the outside knew. But trial dog food made out of various animals, including dogs, and even humans, was outselling all the other brands in the International marketplace. The problem was, it also began making the dogs that were eating it vicious. They began attacking each other in parks and other public places. So the company's researchers in Russia began experimenting with a type of opioid that dulled the dogs' senses, and made them easier to control. That's what worked on Fido, or so we thought. It turned out only to be an inhibitor, not a total cure. But the resultant passivity also meant subjects, both dogs and people, were much less resistant to taking orders, to do absolutely anything, even to their own detriment. Hal decided to apply this process to human food, thinking if he could infiltrate the diets of people everywhere with an addictive, brain-altering substance, they would be more susceptible to subliminal control. His first test subjects were in Miami. One of them escaped, obviously."

I shook my head. I didn't know what to say, except for the obvious sane response: "You're crazy. You're all crazy. Good luck with everything, really. But I'm going home now."

Disgusted and disoriented, I stood back up and began hobbling down the bridge back toward downtown, Jade right behind me, sobbing. I was dazed and dizzy, and bleeding from my neck, but the people I passed were still too busy giggling at their Twitter feeds or taking photos of the river to notice me. I didn't care. I just kept stumbling along with no specific destination in mind, other than my Murphy bed far, far away in Seattle, when I hit a roadblock made out of solid muscle: Brett.

I sighed and looked at his stone cold face and said with stoic resignation, "Just go ahead and do it. I'm in no position to fight back."

Then he obliged and hit me square in the nose, and I went down, unconscious before I even hit the ground.

When I woke up, I looked over to see Brett having steamy sex with Jade. She didn't seem too into it, but then I was pretty groggy, and at first I thought maybe this was one of my twisted dreams. He kept mauling her as she moaned and then they both climaxed and Brett got up and I got a good, close look at his hairy ass. Then I saw her sweaty, nude body laying spread eagle on a platform of some sort, right next to mine. I finally realized this was actually happening.

Still barely conscious, I scanned my surroundings, trying to determine my precise location. I was in a dimly lit basement laboratory. And Jade wasn't just spread eagle, she was strapped to a table. Brett had raped her while she was helplessly bound.

I looked down and noticed I was also nude and strapped down. I feared the worst: I'd also been violated by Brett.

Then I noticed Hal sitting in the corner. He was fully clothed, wearing a lab coat, in fact, and he was holding a very large hypodermic needle, which he set down as he stood up. He went over to Jade and examined her body carefully, holding her eyelids open and staring into them, searching for something.

Then he turned his attention to me. He was still smiling, the bastard. "Hi, Vic," he said as he picked up the needle again, then jabbed the business end right into my scrotum.

I screamed but he didn't react at all. Jade was just lying there, semi-conscious, all sexed-up and sobbing softly, as Brett's contaminated fluids dripped out of her.

"What the fuck?" I said. "What the hell are you doing?"

"I'm injecting you with the antidote," Hal said simply. "Or what we hope is the antidote. We already know you're infected with the virus. Brett just infected Jade, or we assume, since we're not sure semen can transmit the virus as effectively as saliva or blood. We'll soon find out."

"Jade already brought me up to speed on your stupid scheme," I said.

"I know. Brett told me. That's why I let you and Jade go off together alone. He followed you. Jade's purse had been bugged. Sadly, at least for her, my worst suspicions were confirmed. Too bad. I had a feeling she was a double agent, but I hoped I was wrong. Such a fine piece of ass. But now she's as expendable as you are, Vic."

"But what if this antidote works?"

"We'll see. Don't get your hopes up, though. Most likely it won't. Just one last shot, so to speak. The likely scenario is you'll turn into a raving cannibal and Brett here will shoot both you and Jade in the head. But at least he got to have some fun first."

"Even if I turn into a zombie, can't you just let me go back to Seattle? They're all tweeters and stoners. I'll blend right in, trust me."

"Ha, ha. Sorry, Vic. We can't have this mutated virus out on the loose. We've already had to contain it here and there around the world. If this antidote isn't successful, hopefully the one we make with the dog's blood will be. We won't know until we try. That way we won't have to keep blowing heads off, which tends to attract authoritative attention after a while."

"Well, fuck it, then. Fuck everything."

"That's exactly the way I see it, Vic. Glad we're on the same page!"

My biggest worry at the time, should I miraculously survive this situation, was what would I do for a living if I could no longer walk dogs? I was in my fifties and had no money saved for retirement. I was burning through my savings. I had no marketable skills, especially at my age. Maybe it was best I just turned into a zombie. At least then I wouldn't have to worry about where my next meal was coming from.

Suddenly, "Sleepwalk" by Henri René & His Orchestra was playing, somewhere, as my immediate surroundings seemed to swirl down the drain of my brain…

Next thing I knew, I found myself in the Macy's store in downtown Seattle. It was good to be home. Except I was apparently employed as an "elf," working alongside "Santa." Beneath the beard I could tell he was actually Charlie, the actor that had almost made a movie out of my life before he was accused of murder, but then he got off and was free. Except this was the only type of acting job he could score now. I guessed we had both hit the skids.

Then I noticed my good friend and former fuck buddy Monica was sitting on "Santa's" lap. She was naked except for a seasonally correct sweater, and his red pants were down around his shiny black boots. Monica was riding him ferociously as she told him what she wanted for Christmas: a baby. She kept screaming at him to cum inside of her. But she already had a grown kid back East that she never saw anymore. Maybe she wanted another one. The Spawn of Satan. Or Santa. Whatever.

I felt insanely jealous but as a gainfully employed elf, I couldn't do anything. It just wasn't my place to intervene, professionally speaking. All I could do was sit back and watch as if nothing untoward was going on, apologizing to the kids waiting in line for the delay, and to the mothers for exposing their kids to such abhorrent, subversive behavior. It was like being a spokesperson for the Trump administration.

Then I saw a vision of my old pal Doc Schlock sort of glowing in a corner of the store. He motioned for me to come over. But I was afraid to move since I didn't want to get fired. My main qualification for this job was probably my height, and I couldn't think of another gig that would ideally suit my limited stature in society, physically or otherwise. I had that familiar feeling of panic churning in my gut that comes from living in barely sustainable poverty, working humiliating jobs like this one, simply to make ends meet. You have to eat shit just to put food on the table. I hadn't felt that way in real life for a long time, not since I was in my twenties and working as a freelance journalist. But now that my options were dwindling, I felt fortunate to be employed as a department store elf, even if that meant enabling my perverted boss.

Doc was obviously trying to warn me of something, like the Ghost of Christmas Past. In fact, he looked like an apparition, except he was wearing a sharp suit, not a robe or anything. But his body was transparent, almost white, which was odd, since his flesh had been black when he was alive. So yeah, Doc was definitely a spirit, haunting my sorry elf ass. I couldn't make out what he was shouting at me over the sensuous sounds of Monica in heat, though. He just kept waving his arms in alarmed admonition.

Then I looked around and noticed that the popular

performer El Vez, the "Mexican Elvis" (actually Robert Lopez of Seattle, whom I knew slightly), was singing "Santa Claus Is Sometimes Brown" to a large crowd, from a stage in the center of the store. Two buxom, scantily clad burlesque dancers—"the Elvettes"—were go-go dancing on either side of him. The audience consisted of drooling, decaying zombies. Some of them were zombie elves. They turned and saw me, and to my chagrin, the zombie elves started coming my way.

I turned to tell Santa but now he was wearing nothing but a red cap, banging the hell out of Laura, not Monica, who now was making out with Fifi, dressed as Mrs. Claus, though Monica was slowly untying her apron strings in order to get at the holiday goodies beneath her long, fluffy dress. The zombie elves lined up behind "Santa" and then began gang-banging Laura, taking turns. I couldn't help but get turned on, but I dared not try to stop them, much less join them, because the store manager, a dead ringer for Hal, was standing in another corner, browbeating me. The little kids in line were getting restless. Then they began attacking me.

That's when the little kids morphed into little dogs, biting me all over, tearing my elf outfit and then my flesh to shreds as Laura cried out for help, except now it was no longer Laura, it was Jade being assaulted by hordes of zombie elves, all of whom looked like tiny, grinning, ghoulish versions of Brett. Meanwhile, Hal was now drinking Martinis with Dianne, who was decked out in full Nazi regalia, including a cap with a swastika insignia, exactly like Dyanne Thorne in *Ilsa, She Wolf of the SS*. They were both laughing. Then they began fucking in a festive frenzy as El Vez started singing his next number, "Brown Christmas," to the remaining zombie hordes in the audience. Except now both Elvettes were also zombies, and then I noticed El Vez was a zombie, too. I was surrounded by a Christmas-themed orgy of the undead as I was torn apart by little growling dogs that all looked like Fido. I looked up and saw Dianne, still dressed as Ilsa, but topless, beating me, or at least what was left of me, with a whip. Hal was next to her, sipping his Martini. And they laughed and they laughed.

Then I woke up, or at least I opened my eyes, and looked over at poor Jade strapped naked to the lab table, still unconscious, slimy with Brett's bodily fluids, and realized I was probably better off dreaming, because nothing could be weirder than my new waking reality. So I just went back to sleep.

Chapter Seven
HOUSTON, YOU HAVE A PROBLEM

I awoke to the sound of "Drums-a-Go-Go" by the Hollywood Persuaders, which I hadn't heard in a while, at least not since I left Seattle, but at first I couldn't figure out if it was coming from outside or inside my head.

When I saw Laura and Jade, both wearing bikinis, go-go dancing next to a little vintage turntable resting on a tripod, on which played a 45 of that very song, I realized I must still be dreaming. Except I wasn't. It didn't matter anymore. The lines between fantasy and reality had been blurred beyond designation by now.

I looked down and noticed I was wearing a blue aloha shirt, thin white slacks, and *huaraches.*

When they noticed I was awake, they both stopped dancing, looked at me, and said in cheery unison, "Hi Vic!"

Then they ran over and kissed me, one on each cheek. I felt like Elvis in *Blue Hawaii.*

"We figured you needed a change of clothes," Jade said.

"Yeah, the others were all bloody," Laura said. "How do you feel?"

"Depends. Where are we?"

"Houston," Jade said.

"Then shitty."

I noticed we were beside a pool, which was next to a nifty midcentury modern ranch-style house. Then I started to feel the sun on my skin, which began to itch. I really, really, *really* hate the sun, as you must know by now. I'm allergic to it, I think. It was humid, too. I smelled barbecue in the breeze and the neighbors were shouting at some kind of sporting event on TV. Despite the company and music, I felt immediately out of place. Yeah, we were in Texas, all right.

"I think I'm missing a few pieces of my mind," I said. "Last I remember, I was strapped nude to a lab table, next to you, Jade. Brett had just had his way with you."

"Yes, that all happened," Jade whispered. "Just play along, Vic."

"Play along with what? The music?"

"You recognize your own collection, Vic?" Jade said. "We had some of your stuff brought here, to make you feel at home."

"Just don't freak out," Laura said. "Things are not what they seem."

"Are they ever?"

As if right on queue, a little dog that looked just like Fido came running out of the house. Except it wasn't Fido. Not the one I knew, anyway. Same mixed breed, but he was the wrong color, more brown than black. I was bad when it came to people, but I always remembered details about dogs and cats. I guess because they mattered more to me.

"That's not Fido," I said.

Laura slapped me across the cheek, the same one she had just kissed. "Shush, Hal's coming. Don't tell him we switched dogs."

"What?"

Then Hal and Brett walked out of the house. Hal was smiling, and Brett wasn't. At least some things were still the same.

"Drums-a-Go-Go" had ended, and was replaced with another super-rare but ultra-cool vintage instrumental tune called "Firewater," by The Premiers. Laura and Jade resumed dancing like they were beach bunnies just kicking it at a 1950s pool party. Apparently they, or someone, had raided my precious collection of 45s, many of them culled from Bop Street Records back in Seattle, right there in Ballard. I'd spent a lot of time and money building up my stash, and they weren't easily replaced. Somehow I deduced that was part of the point. In a way, they were holding my records for ransom. But ransom for what?

Then I realized the whole, insidious, nefarious purpose: *control.*

Speak of the Devil: Hal casually walked up to me, handed me a drink in a tiki mug, replete with a little fuchsia-colored umbrella, and said, "Aloha, Vic! Welcome to Houston!"

Now, as you know, I never refuse a free drink, so I accepted the tiki mug, and took a sip. It was something with juice and rum, very strong and sour, so I kept sipping as Brett stood there with his arms folded, staring at nothing, the girls kept dancing, and Hal kept smiling.

"How did I get here? And why am I here?" I finally asked.

"The eternal questions, Vic," Hal said. "But I'm afraid I can't help you with these existential dilemmas facing all of us. We must each learn to cope in our own way."

I nodded wearily, so tired of his bullshit. Instead I tried to draw a direct line between my last memory and my current state of semi-consciousness. "Last thing I remember, a department store Santa and his gang of zombie elves were gang-banging Laura while little dogs were tearing me apart and her mother was whipping me, dressed like a Nazi, but topless."

Hal raised his eyebrows with a shrug, inhaled then exhaled a little breath, and said, "Well, I can't help you with that either, Vic. But perhaps I can help you fill in a few other blanks in that strange little head of yours."

Just then, Dianne walked up beside Hal and slipped her arm around his. She was popping out of a skimpy bikini. Maybe I was dead, after all. And if this were Hell, what could Heaven possibly possess as a tempting counter-offer?

"Hi, Vic," she said eerily, as if all of this made sense. Maybe it did, at least per her twisted sense of logic. Plus, since she was now hooked up with Hal, whom I assumed was her nemesis, she obviously knew something I didn't. Most people did, it seemed.

Besides the bikini, she was wearing a floppy sun hat, big sunglasses, and high heels. She smirked when she said to me, "Can I help you fill in any holes?" My mind was easier to read than the back of a cereal box.

"Let's all go to my favorite local tiki bar and catch up there!" Hal said. "We have much to celebrate!"

(You may have also noticed this tiki-theme running through the narrative. Don't worry, I've noticed it too. Just in case you thought you were crazy or something. It made everything feel so much more exotic (not that it was exactly mundane anyway), like I was on vacation or safari or something. More like "something." Now back to our story. Mine, anyway.)

"Houston has a tiki bar?" I said, as if that prospect were somehow inconceivable.

"Lei Low," Dianne said.

"I'm trying to," I said. "But shit keeps happening."

"That's the name of the bar, dumbass."

"I wouldn't think Texas would be a tiki kinda place, though they do have lots of sun 'n' palm trees 'n' shit. And plenty of reasons to drink, I imagine. Like everyone else."

"Houston does have a lot of great bars," she confirmed. "I should know."

"Yeah? How's that? You got a vacation home here, too? I hope this isn't it, if so."

"I was raised here, dumbass."

"I did not know that."

"There are a lot of things you don't know, Vic. Hence, you're a dumbass."

I raised my tiki mug and said, "I hereby declare you the winner of the International Miss Understatement

Contest."

"I was actually runner up for Miss Houston."

"Oh yeah? What year, nineteen fifty-seven?"

Then she threw the contents of her cocktail glass into my face. I wiped then licked it off my own hand. The fluid blended well with the one I was drinking.

"Now, now," Hal said. "Vic is a just bit confused, and no wonder. I bet he didn't expect to wake up here after our last encounter. If at all."

"I thought you were all playing on opposing teams," I said, looking at Dianne and Laura. They had put on one of my old albums now, a lounge collection by Jackie Gleason, since they had stopped dancing and required something long-playing to accompany their current activity. I wondered what else they had plundered from my Ballard studio apartment. I hoped my cat was okay, at least.

I didn't have to worry about him anymore once I walked in and saw Doc lounging on a plush sofa, licking his balls, or where his balls once were. I missed my own, too.

"We just wanted to make you comfortable here, Vic!" Hal said, echoing the girls and slapping me on the shoulder. "We've relocated you to Houston, at least for now. Then we're on to Costa Rica, where it's even hotter and sunnier!"

Okay, *now* we were officially in Hell. Though at least this little slice of it had air-conditioning, an absolute necessity year-round in Texas. At least for weather wimps like me.

"I *hate* the fucking sun, that's why I moved to Seattle from California!" I said. But fuck the sun and the heat and the human race. I went over to Doc and picked him up and hugged him tight. He was obviously traumatized, but settled down quickly in my arms. Fido's stunt double was running around barking because nobody was paying him any attention. I felt sorry for him, too. Fuck these god damn homo sapiens. Well, most of 'em.

Oblivious to their surroundings, Laura and Jade had

stripped out of their bikinis and were now eating each other out just outside the door. But before I even had a chance to adjust the leaking bulge in my white slacks, I heard moaning and screaming coming from the bedroom, or one of them.

I put Doc down and ran to the room and kicked open the door. There was Fifi, entertaining four dirty, naked men that looked like they hadn't had a bath since Esther Williams was a big box-office draw. They were drooling and slobbering and ejaculating all over her, penetrating every orifice with their filthy members, but she appeared to be loving it, wiping their scummy semen all over her body, reveling in the defilement. One of her zombified lovers looked over at me and grinned. His eyes were red and his teeth were rotten. His skin was sallow and his bare, bony frame was hairy and gross.

Instinctively, I reached down to grip my own burgeoning boner when Hal slapped me on the shoulder and snapped me back to reality. Or rather, his version of it.

Shutting the door on the salacious scenario, he said, "That's another experiment in progress, Vic. The idea is, if we pump more infected semen into a body, will it produce more immediately visible results?"

"All in the service of mankind. How honorable."

"Now you're getting it!"

"Looks more like a *sex*periment."

"That's very witty, Vic," Hal said dryly. "Mind if I borrow it?"

"How did you make Fifi consent to this?"

"Consent? Hell, Vic, Fifi *volunteered*! Well, sort of. Fifi has been working for me this whole time, keeping an eye on Jade. Fifi was, shall we say, under the influence of certain narcotics, which I selectively administered. Anyway, Fifi's reports from the field are what made me suspicious about Jade's true motives. But the antidote we gave Jade worked, probably because semen contains a very low level of the virus. Good to know. So we made a new deal, and I extended her contract."

"Which is?"

"She's going to help me kill David."

"That's okay with Laura?"

"It was Laura's idea. She hates the fucker."

"*Hates* him. Wants him dead. Her own father."

"He used to molest her as a kid."

"What?" This plot had more twists than Chubby Checker in a pretzel factory.

"That's what she told me, anyway. It's a sick world full of sick people, Vic. But we're working on the cure. Now c'mon, let's go. I'll buy you an even better drink and answer all your questions. Except the ones about the meaning of Life. That's a little outside my range of expertise. Though I'm doing my research, as you can see."

"Can't I watch? I mean I've always been curious about the mysteries of the Universe and all that jazz. I'd like to see how it comes out."

"Not now. Be patient, Vic. You'll learn the secrets of Life, and Death, soon enough. With my help."

"Damn. Thanks."

"No problem!"

At least my cat was okay, relatively speaking. It was good to see him, even out of a comfortable context. I just worried about my landlady's condition. But I didn't have time to think about that, either. Nothing I could do about it at the moment, anyway. Everyone was on their own.

The Lei Low Tiki Bar was part of a mini-strip mall on Main Street. Or that's what the street sign said, anyway. I wondered if it was the same Main Street that The Shameful Tiki was on, way back up in Vancouver, and it extended all the way down here to Houston. One long street lined with tiki bars. That was the route of my life these days.

Honestly, I had no idea exactly where I was, sans any frame of geographical reference, since the only town I'd ever visited in Texas was Austin, and that was years ago when I was in my twenties, researching an article for this New York rag. I covered a lot of New Wave bands back in the day. I was probably there reporting on the local punk scene, but frankly I don't remember much because I was drunk most of the time. Though I knew it was destroying my liver and whatever was left of my brain, my alcohol-induced amnesia was turning out to be my saving grace. Now if only I could just forget the rest of it, like I mean *everything*, I'd be a much happier man. At least I was well on my way to a blissfully permanent blackout.

The Lei Low was small, cozy and densely decorated with assorted Pop Polynesian artifacts, much like The Shameful Tiki. It was starting to seem like the United States was packed with tiki bars coast to coast, just like back in the postwar era. The truth was I just seemed to gravitate toward the few that were left, regardless of my occupation at any given time. Perhaps it was a psychosomatic compass, leading me from tiki bar to tiki bar, so I was constantly ensconced in faux-tropical, retro-kitschy aesthetics, intoxicated both by my environment and its liquid assets, immunized against the adverse affects of the real world.

As usual, Brett stood silent guard as Hal, Dianne and I sat in a rear booth. We'd left Jade and Laura behind, and I doubt they even noticed we'd left, preoccupied by passion. Likewise filthy Fifi and her hideous horde of humping hobos.

Dianne was still mad at me, and wouldn't even give me the courtesy of eye contact. I didn't care. She'd put on a flimsy flower pattern dress but left on the high heels, leaving plenty of tan flesh exposed, and that's all the communication I'd ever need from her. Well, unless I got to bang her again, but I had the feeling I'd blown all future options in that regard.

After we sat down, and she crossed her gams and noticed me looking down at her red-painted toes in those pumps, she kicked me in the shin. I guess I'd indeed completely alienated her with my little off-the-cuff wisecrack. I had no idea she was so sensitive about her age, especially since she was several years younger than I was. But then my behavior was often pretty juvenile, which shaved off a few years in my favor, at least per the perception of more mature observers.

Hal ordered a 1944 Mai Tai for Two (a house specialty) at the bar, and fortunately it was meant only for me. Then he ordered two other tropical drinks for Dianne and himself. Brett didn't drink at all, ever, apparently. I was glad about that. I'd already seen him in action, under the insidious influence of whatever version of the virus he'd been infected with. I didn't want to see him drunk, too. Though maybe it would loosen him up a bit. Not worth the risk, probably.

"Okay, Hal, lay it on me," I said, sipping my Man Tai, the flaming crouton singeing the tip of my nose. I had become so accustomed to pain, physical and otherwise, that I didn't even notice. My nose hairs could've caught fire and I would've just doused them with booze, exploding my whole stupid fucking face.

I noticed they were playing Les Baxter's *Jungle Jazz* album on the sound system, so there was that, at least.

"What is this about you hating the sun?" Hal said. "That doesn't make any sense! Everyone loves the sun!"

"I dig it dark and cold," I said. "Like my heart. But I'm not here to discuss my atmospheric preferences. What happened since I woke up strapped to a lab table somewhere in Minneapolis?"

"Actually, that was here in Texas. You really don't remember? Wow. Interesting. Must be yet another side effect of the stronger version of the virus."

"Why didn't you just let me die and get it over with?"

"We wanted to give you a few hours to see if the antidote worked first."

"And it did?"

"No, you just went into a little coma, during which time we transported you here, and then injected you with the new, improved antidote, using the blood of a certain dog."

"So you found Fido," I said, going along with the subterfuge which Laura and Jade had obviously rigged. I assumed they were operating undercover, as double agents, explaining the facade of collaboration with a sworn enemy. Then again, maybe they'd been yanking my chain this whole time. I really had no idea. But I was worried about the *real* Fido. Meantime, I played the game by the rules as currently enforced.

"Yes, we located the dog, with very little trouble," Hal said. "In fact, David gave him right up as soon as we got here. We've reached a truce, of sorts. By now you must know we had a disagreement about the future of our joint venture. But now that an antidote to the virus has been found, we can proceed with the original plan."

"Which is?"

"Turning dog meat into dog food. Mass production, recycling resources for the good of the environment. Plus profits though the roof. And after that, we move on to the next phase: human flesh for humans."

I spit out a mouthful of Mai Tai, right on Dianne's cleavage. "I can lick it off," I said, but she slapped me. It turned me on, but then I didn't really have an "off" switch, so I was always horny by default.

"Fuck you," she said.

"I'm always ready, baby," I said.

"Settle down, everyone," Hal said.

I ignored her and asked him, "Um, what exactly are you talking about, Hal? You're actually going to mainstream cannibalism as a mass-produced consumer item?"

"Yes, why not? I mean, we won't *tell* anyone that. It won't be part of the ad campaign, of course. People are consuming and digesting all kinds of chemicals all the time, and if they knew what they were, they'd completely panic. So this type of distribution is already in place, and has been for decades. We'll just pitch our products as a new, affordable brand of meat, for animals as well as people, while also clandestinely recycling the dead flesh of animals and people. Death gives back to Life, for once."

"So you really expect this product to take off? Seriously?"

"It will be like Spam, only much, much tastier. I mean, does anyone really know what's in Spam? Or a hot dog, for that matter? They don't want to know, Vic. They just like how it tastes. That's the mentality of the First World consumer these days. And even Second and Third World, if given the opportunity. The world as a whole is vastly over-populated. Climate change is rapidly spoiling the planet. Human beings need to be contained as a species before they inflict irreparable damage on our shared space in the Universe. We, the so-called Elite, need to be proactive as well as protective, and since politicians and scientists have their own selfish agendas, we businessmen and entrepreneurs are providing a compromise solution, without revealing any of the facts, which only complicate the natural flow of things, anyway."

"David is cool with all this now?"

"He will be, when I have a chance to explain it to him. Right now we're united by the combined effort to stop the mutated virus. Once I win him over with that, we can proceed as partners, like always."

"So nobody else knows about any of this. Except me."

"Only the right people in the right places. And for now, that includes you. But you'll be dead soon, so it doesn't matter, ultimately."

"So you're like a James Bond villain, right, spilling your whole scheme to me because you think I won't live to report back."

"Yes! I'm like Goldfinger. But you're not anything like James Bond, and you have nobody to report back to, so that's where your analogy falls apart. You're actually going to die. Unlike Bond. Unless you find another actor to play you, like he keeps doing."

That certainly sent a chill down my spine. "But I thought you gave me an antidote to a virus I didn't even know I had? I mean, what were my symptoms, even?"

"You ate a ham sandwich, Vic."

"No, I didn't. No fucking way." I began feeling nauseous just thinking about the possibility of eating some poor, innocent pig, unintentionally or not.

"Yes, you did. I hand-fed it to you back in the lab. I have it on tape somewhere. You were under the influence of the virus, and also under my control. I simply hypnotized you to forget. But since I know you don't normally eat meat, yet you ate a ham sandwich on command, without hesitation, you must be infected. Plus your eyes were red."

"They're often red. I drink."

"Not *this* red."

"How can I believe something I can't even remember?"

"You've suffered alcoholic blackouts before, Vic. Like in Chicago."

"Hey, how do you know that?"

"I have friends in many places, Vic. Even here." Hal nodded toward the bar.

I turned to notice some mean-looking dudes sitting on stools, with rods sticking out of their pants, in defiance of Texas's open carry law, which excluded bars, and for good reason: gun butts were even more unsightly than ass-cracks.

"So you're planning to kill me anyway, after all this," I said.

"Eventually. In a time and place of my own choosing, once you've fully fulfilled your purpose."

"You're a fucking sociopath," I said. "You should run

for office. You might wind up the fucking president one day."

Hal smiled and said, "One step at a time."

God, I was so sick of people. Let them devour and choke on each other. I was so done.

Then I noticed a group of patrons at the table across from us, obviously loaded, having a lot of fun, with no idea that their doom was being discussed a few feet away. They were young, healthy, good-looking, and loud. Two older women joined them, everyone kissed each other, and the loving warmth was truly touching. I nearly cried. This type of familial camaraderie was something I'd never experienced in my own life.

"Excuse me," I said to Hal, abruptly rising to go greet the strangers. Then rudely interrupting their revelry, I introduced myself, and they actually asked me to join them.

Their names were Eric, Aaron, Mary Lee, Kristen, Andrew, Amy, Tiffany, Jefferey, Robin, Mina, and Carol. They were all lifelong Houstonians and proud Texans. And bawdy as hell.

Mina was the mother of Eric, who was married to Mary Lee, and Aaron, who was married to Kristen. Carol was the mother of Amy, who was married to Andrew, and Tiffany, who was married to Jefferey. Robin was their older cousin, and single, but she had a kid, who was being watched with everyone else's kids by someone named Uncle Tommy.

At first they wanted to talk about sports, asking about my perceived allegiance to the Mariners and the Seahawks, but when I confessed I wasn't sure which sport those teams played, or what city they were from, they moved on to other topics that were actually within my limited wheelhouse. We chatted about the weather and movies for a while, sidestepped politics and religion, and eventually wound up on the subject of family. By this time I had completely forgotten about Hal and Dianne.

"So what is the secret of having a family?" I asked no

one in particular.

"You really don't know?" Aaron said, and they all laughed.

"That's the funnest part!" Eric said.

"It's the not-sleeping part that isn't as much fun," Kristen said.

"But still worth it," Mary Lee added.

"Absolutely," Tiffany said.

"Eventually," Amy chimed in.

"I didn't lose any sleep when the kids were born," Andrew said.

"Me, either," said Jefferey.

"Because we did all the work!" Amy said.

"Not all of it!" Eric said in the males' defense.

"Yeah, we woke you up to do it, so you couldn't sleep later!" Aaron said, and then they all busted up laughing.

I laughed too, partly at my own expense, since they'd missed my point, so after the mirth died down, I said, "No. I have child-free sex all the time."

Then they all looked at me with humorless expressions.

"You're a sinner?" Robin said. "You now what they say: love the sin but hate the sinner! Ain't that it, or did I mix it up again?"

More raucous laughter.

"That's okay, honey," Robin said. "We're all sinners."

"Not as bad as me," I said.

"We know, you're from sin-y Seattle!" Aaron said, and they all started laughing again.

Mina and Carol began feeling sorry for me, and since I was sitting between them, they each gave me a hug.

"You're just looking for a family, aren't you?" Carol said with genuine sympathy.

"I guess," I said, choking up.

"Don't worry," Mina said. "Your true family will find *you*."

"But I'm so old now," I said.

"It's never too late to start over," Carol said.

"That's right," said Mina. "You just never know what's waiting for you just around the corner."

Right then two hulking cowboys armed with shotguns walked in and opened fire, immediately blowing away the badasses at the bar that worked for Hal, before apparently training their sights on Hal himself. I ducked under the table, and so did Hal and Dianne and everyone else in the joint. Except for the folks at my table. They all had their guns drawn, and they returned fire, eventually driving the two cowboys back out of the bar. Brett was also shooting at them, and he hit both, but didn't kill them. They ran out and I heard the screeching tires of a getaway truck mixed in with all the screaming. Brett chased after them, from what I could hear, shooting at them as they fled, and then hopping in his own car in hot pursuit.

Back inside, bottles and bottles of premium booze had been shattered, their precious contents pouring all over the bullet-ridden bamboo bar and tables and walls. Innocent patrons were bleeding from wounds suffered in the crossfire. They'd probably be okay. They could get patched up, via a transfusion maybe. But what a senseless waste of good rum. You couldn't mop it up and put it back where it belonged, unlike guts.

Once the smoke had cleared, I stood up and looked over to see if Hal and Dianne were safe. He was. But she was lying dead in his arms, blood seeping from big gaping holes in her tanned, bountiful chest. Hal didn't look sad or even upset. He looked determined.

Wrong place, wrong time, wrong company. This had obviously been a bold hit on Hal, with collateral, incidental damage suffered instead of the actual target being taken out, but who was behind this? David? Laura and Jade? Mickey Rourke? Mafia? CIA? KGB? Some player I didn't know about yet?

Then I looked over as my new Texas friends put away their pistols. Carol actually blew smoke from the tip of her mean-looking gat. I'd carried a .38 for years but that's the extent of my gun knowledge—I'm not an expert about anything but women and booze, and even then I take a lot of wild guesses.

Carol winked at me.

"Don't mess with Texas," Mina said.

I made a mental note of it.

Chapter Eight
DEAD STATE

What quickly became known as "The Texas Tiki Bar Massacre" spread throughout local and then worldwide media, even though that was technically a slight exaggeration, since only Dianne actually perished, as tragic as that was. Five people gradually recovered in the hospital. Best of all, my new Texas family survived, totally unscathed. In fact, all of their bullets were "warning shots," only damaging some tiki mugs and bottles of booze. That must've been the "massacre" part.

After the cops came and left, they actually wanted to bring me home with them and basically adopt me, but Hal—who apparently was well known to local authorities, released immediately after questioning, above any suspicion—insisted I go back home with him to look in on "the girls," which is when I suddenly realized that Hal's place might've been the first target of the hired gunmen, and Laura, Jade and Fifi collateral casualties along this trail of carnage. And the horny hobo freaks, too, but they were already undead, anyway. I mourned who they were before that, though.

Anyway, anxious to check on their welfare, I accompanied Hal back to his home, where Brett was standing on the front stoop, arms folded, looking grim, though it was hard to read anything into his expression since he always looked that way.

As soon as we walked in the door and flipped on the light, we knew it was bad. Very bad.

Laura and Jade were lying naked and bloody on the

patio just outside the rear sliding door. We ran over to them but neither was responsive. Then Hal ran into the bedroom.

While he was briefly gone, Jade began to stir, jump-starting my heart. I gently lifted up her limp body into my arms. Barely conscious, she pulled my face close to hers and whispered to me cryptically, "The toucans are not what they seem." Then she died. I assumed her last words were the product of delirium, and dismissed them. For the moment, anyway.

I kissed her cold lips then inhaled her final breath. Laura was already beyond any sensation whatsoever. I was in a state of shock, too stunned and sad to cry or scream.

Hal had returned by then. I could read *his* expression. Then I looked around and saw the still body of Fido's doppelganger. They even killed the dog. Perhaps that was the whole point.

This was the true massacre.

Then suddenly I thought of one other occupant that hadn't been accounted for: Doc, my cat. I stood up and began calling his name, my already moist eyes leaking down my cheeks.

Then I heard a frightened meow and Doc came running towards me from beneath a sofa. I picked him up and covered him with kisses, pressing him to my chest. He licked me back, purring with relief, but shaking with fear. I let him go and ran back to hide under the sofa. I wanted to join him.

"It's time to go," Hal said.

"And just leave them here?" I said.

"They're dead, Vic. I mean really dead. Not undead. Come on, let's go. Leave the cat."

"No fucking way."

I felt the hard steel of Brett's gun on the back of my skull. If Doc hadn't been there, needing me to save him, I would've just leaned back and told him to pull the trigger and release me from this kennel of horrors.

"I am not abandoning my cat," I said. "So you'll have to shoot both of us." Then I cringed, praying he wouldn't call my bluff.

"That would be a waste," Hal said. "You can't bring your cat to Costa Rica, sorry. And I need you alive for now. We're still monitoring your symptoms. Or I am, anyway. Now let's go. I need to leave the country until the smoke clears."

"No. Not without Doc. He's the only family I got. If you hadn't catnapped him, he wouldn't even be here."

Hal sighed. "Look, Vic. The cat will be safe here. I'll have someone look in on him and take care of him while we're gone, okay?"

"Yeah, like you did with the girls?"

Hal hardened his gaze, not smiling for once. "This wasn't part of the plan, Vic. Not originally, anyway. But plans were made to change on the fly. The gunmen were after me. The girls were just in the wrong place at the wrong time. And they wanted to send a message, in the worst possible way."

"Who exactly is 'they'?"

"My guess is David's faction. He fooled me. I thought we were partners again, converging on the same path forward. But, apparently not. So now it's back to war. Fine with me. War is my natural element. I thrive in conflict."

"Don't really give a shit about your self-analysis, pally. Just let me and the cat go. I promise not to say anything." Of course, those were the famous last words of many dead people throughout history, so I admittedly regretted it.

Hal's creepy smile made a comeback. "No. The reason I brought your cat and records here is because I was trying to be nice. And I know those are possessions of yours that are unique and irreplaceable. I wanted you to feel at home here, even though it's only a pitstop on the way to our real destination."

"I get why the cat. Why the fucking records? I can

always buy more."

"Because you see your life as a movie, and it needs an appropriate soundtrack. I was simply accommodating your dementia."

For a moment I was worried he could actually monitor my thoughts, since "Drums-a-Go-Go" had been stuck in my head lately, as you know, because I told you, but I didn't want to give him too much credit. Or any ideas. So I just said, "Thanks. And while you're being so gracious, I'd like to go back home to Seattle now."

"That's never going to happen, Vic. I thought maybe I could make you a home away from home here in Houston, at least while you're still alive. But now even that plan has changed. Such is life. Poetry in motion. Sometimes fucked-up poetry. Like Bukowski."

"Bukowski wrote great poetry. The best. The only poetry I ever read, in fact. So fuck you."

"I'm not saying it wasn't good, but it was crudely expressed and often inelegant, compared to, say, a Shakespeare sonnet. He was the bard of lowlifes. Like you. Plus on a construction level, it had no rhyme or reason. Literally. Like much of life."

I sighed. Arguing with this asshole about anything was a dead end. "Just let us go, man. This is your home, not ours."

Hal shook his head. "It's just a house. Property. My home base is in Minneapolis, but I'm hardly ever there. I own real estate all over this ball of shit called Earth, Vic. I was going to let you have it, as a reward. But now, due to unforeseen circumstances—and the most effective catalysts in life are always unpredicted—it's nothing more than a tomb. The cat has outlived his usefulness, too."

I was so very tired of Hal's god damn God complex, and was about to tell him so, when Brett pointed his gun at the sofa, obviously intent on shooting right through it, hitting Doc. So instead I turned and hit Brett square in the face as hard as I could. Of course, he didn't even flinch.

Despite my Hunter-esque fear and loathing for just about everything at that moment, I remained resolute. "You kill the cat, I'm not going anywhere. Like I said. Just kill us both here and now and leave our bodies piled with the rest of these rotting pieces of dead flesh you don't give a shit about. I guess they all outlived their usefulness, too. Funny how only assholes like you are left standing when the smoke clears, and you're the reason everything blew up in the first place. What a fucking world. You're right. It is a ball of shit. And you're the flies feeding off of it."

Hal just shook his head dismissively. What a patronizing prick. "The cops will be here soon, Vic, so we don't have any more time to swap metaphors right now. They bought my story back at the bar, but this mess coming right on its heels would require too much complex explanation and just waste more precious time, one commodity I can't buy or sell, making it the most valuable. So let's go. *Now.*"

Brett was still pointing at Doc, straight through the sofa.

"Okay," I said, only relenting because a workable compromise had just popped into my head. "Here's the new deal: I know of a place where I can leave Doc while we're gone, where I won't have to worry about him. Otherwise I wouldn't be of any use to you, because I'd be too preoccupied with his health and safety." It was true. One reason of many I gave up being a full-time detective was I hated leaving Doc alone at home for hours, days, or weeks at a time. As far as I was concerned, the spirit of the human Doc inhabited this little furry form, and nothing or nobody but Nature could ever take him away from me.

"You really know people around here, Vic?" Hal asked, considering the proposition. "People you can trust, I mean. Which obviously excludes present company."

"Yeah. Extended family, you might say." Fortunately

my gun-toting adoptive family from the tiki bar had left me their contact info.

Hal mulled it over, then said, "Deal. We'll take the carrier we used to transport him, and drop him off with a note. But no interaction. We can't afford the risk or the delay."

I tried to continue negotiating, but Brett moved from the sofa and stuck the business end of his gun in my mouth. I looked down at the dead bodies of Laura, Jade, and poor little Fake Fido, then imagined the gorily grotesque scenario in the bedroom, and relented with an acquiescent nod, biding my time till I had the opportunity to get all John Wick on both their psycho asses.

Meantime, I just wanted to solve one urgent mystery: Who killed Laura Palmer?

I left Doc in his crate with a note addressed to Mina and Carol, thanking them and promising I'd be back in touch soon with further instructions, and hopefully retrieval on my way back to Seattle. One of them lived in Pearland, the other in Friendswood, two Houston suburbs right down the road from each other. I didn't know which lived at which address they'd given me, so I put both their names on the envelope and had Brett drive us to one of their homes via GPS. I didn't even know or care which since both ladies seemed trustworthy, and all suburbs looked alike to me, anyway.

Naturally I'd left my vintage record collection behind at Hal's house, since none of that material crap meant anything to me anymore. Only life itself mattered. My sudden spiritual awakening was well timed, since after Hal hit a few buttons on his cellphone, the house exploded behind us within thirty seconds of our departure. Out of desperation, I was assuming he'd left my DVD collection intact back at my pad in Seattle, since that was way too much to transport easily. I didn't own as many LPs and 45s, mostly CDs, which were relatively disposable. Hal was right. I cherished my old records, now gone for good. "Drums-a-Go-Go" was still playing in my head, though. It was safest there, I figured. And I might not live to watch my DVDs and Blu Rays again, anyway, which really saddened me. I just wanted to donate my collection to Scarecrow Video before I died, but I doubted I'd have the opportunity to draw up a will on the way to my certain doom. At least Doc would have a good home. That's all that ultimately mattered to me, even though I already missed him so much I had stomach cramps.

We were silent in the car on the way to Hal's private jet inside his private hangar located at his private airfield just outside the relatively public city of Houston. Along with the recently deceased, I started thinking about Raven, for some reason. She was the bi-sexual burlesque dancer that wound up in prison for her involvement with a corrupt Seattle cop running a prostitution/porn racket, which also ultimately sucked Charlie and me into its nasty, nihilistic web of deception, decadence, and death. In fact, that's how I landed in Seattle, the only positive byproduct of that sordid affair. Raven had been a victim of sexual abuse while in college, and it twisted her perspective. In my mind, she was totally innocent of all charges. I even said so at her trial. But it was to no avail. She was sentenced for aiding and abetting not only dirty cops, but serial killers, since these monsters were selling underground "snuff" tapes of their victims engaged in various acts of carnality before being murdered on film. Raven had unwillingly starred in a few of them as a sexual partner, shown to the jury, who were obviously horrified as well as a little titillated by the indisputable physical evidence of her participation in these lurid events (or at least I was). In any case, she was sentenced to prison, and soon after, she was found dead in her cell. She'd hung herself with her own massive bra.

Now several more women with whom I'd been

intimate were dead. Flesh that I had enjoyed was now so much worm food. Mine would be too, maybe sooner than later, given the rapid progress of current events. But I promised their spirits to avenge their deaths—even Dianne's, regardless of her complicity—one way or another, including Fake Fido's, while rescuing the real Fido in the process. If he was still with us. Maybe he was better off somewhere over that fabled Rainbow Bridge, hanging out with all my ill-fated ex-girlfriends, far away from this tragic magic show called Life on Earth, full of tricks distracting you from the ultimate truth: it's all just an illusion, and any of us could disappear at any time, for no good reason other than our number happened to come up suddenly. Just like on that HBO series *The Leftovers*. Except I felt more like the main course.

Poor Fido. He was so fucked. Just like all the loves of my life. Right now, it seemed the only person left alive that was actually on Fido's side was me. So I had to stay alive for his sake. As well as Doc's. And Monica's, my only true human friend. Too bad I couldn't have set her up with Laura or Jade or Fifi. Or all three. Maybe then they'd all still be alive, lesbian-ing it up down in a Portland love nest. Or then again, maybe Monica would be dead now, too.

Trying to unravel all these threads was giving me a migraine, so I decided to make it contagious.

"Hal, did David know you were fucking Dianne?" I asked from the back seat, where Brett was sitting next to me, ready to break my neck if I made a wrong move.

"No," Hal said simply, concentrating on the dark road, or something dark, anyway. It was the middle of the night, still and quiet and stinky as roadkill.

"You sure?" I said. "I mean, maybe that's why he tried to kill you."

"Oh, please. He didn't even love Dianne."

"Did you?"

"Fuck, no. Love is nothing but a liability, Vic, you

should know that by now. I knew she was screwing me, but she was such a good lay, I let her, at least literally speaking. Up until I could no longer afford it. I'd hoped David had really changed his mind and was back on my side, along with Dianne. Plus I knew Dianne eventually wanted to knock off David so she could assume power of his empire, without me as a partner. None of it could actually work, of course, since I knew what they were up to, but they didn't know I knew, or maybe they did, so they jumped the gun, so to speak. For whatever reason, they decided to make their play, and it simply backfired in my favor. Not without some subversive orchestration on my part, of course."

"Really? Hm." My detective instincts were kicking in, like an acute case of indigestion. "It does seem rather coincidental David put a hit out on you, but wound up taking out his own ally."

Hal actually stopped the car cold, and pulled over to the shoulder. It was so black and desolate outside we might as well have been on the moon, which was shining overhead, full and bright, very werewolf-friendly.

Hal turned around and gave me a hard look, without smiling. I was afraid he was going to ask me, "Want to see something *really* scary?" But instead he calmly inquired, "What precisely are you insinuating, Vic?"

"It wasn't a comment. It was a question in the form of an observation. I mean, how did David know you were at the Lei Low?"

"I told him to meet us there."

"And so he did."

"I'm not sure about that yet. But that's the most obvious conclusion."

"Who else would it be?"

"You tell me, Vic."

"I have no idea, man. I'm just along for the ride. Like, literally."

"You're the detective. Or you once were. Think about

it. I know you've been wondering about this, too. So lay it on me, Sherlock. Who else would want me dead, in your professional opinion?"

I tried not to feel flattered, since I knew that was his intention, an obvious manipulation device, but the fact was, I had been giving this whole thing considerable thought. "You've probably made a lot of enemies in your time." I said. "I know I'm in that club now, too. But it wasn't me, obviously. So it had to be someone else that was tracking your whereabouts, maybe someone with inside knowledge."

Hal nodded. "True. Good job. David could always locate me easily, via my cellphone if nothing else, since he had my number, literally. So yes, I agree. He tried to hit me at the tiki bar, with or without Dianne's knowledge, but she's out of the picture now anyway, which is good for both of us, whether he even realized or planned it that way or not. But what about the girls back at the house? Who did them? Same shooters, you think?"

"That would be my guess, sure. But remember, I'm such an ace detective I walk dogs for a living."

Hal looked at me with that humorless glaze again. "Think harder, Vic. I concur it was an inside job, but just how far inside did it go? As far inside as you could get, perhaps? The way I see it, Vic, and I'm no expert like you, but maybe it was only *meant* to look like it was someone else, the most obvious culprit, one with a provable motive, for the cops' sake. And yours, just so I could get you out of that house before it went kablooey, and extend some semblance of trust in me."

Then it hit me. I felt light-headed with disgust and disdain. And suddenly much more insecure in my own safety. "Wait. *You* killed Laura and Jade and Fifi and the bums and the dog?"

"Yes! Ding-ding-ding! You take first prize, Vic! But then, no. Not directly. Brett actually did the dirty deed, since that's his purpose in life, kowtowing to my bidding. Right, Brett?"

Brett didn't respond, but then he never did.

Hal took his silence as affirmation, then kept confessing, like he was grateful for the chance to come clean for once, even to a dead man, or one marked for death, anyway. "See, Brett's been one step behind and ahead of you all along, Vic. You should be thankful. Who do you think helped Laura drag you out of Dianne's burning house in Seattle? Or helped Jade carry you from that bar in Vancouver? Why, your trusty friend here, Brett."

"Friends don't let friends kill friends," I said, barely able to breathe, claustrophobic with dread.

"Jade and Laura weren't your friends, Vic. Neither was Dianne. They were just using you as a buffer. They had all outlived their usefulness to me as well. So I set up David for the hits."

"So you could wipe out all your enemies in one foul sweep, without anyone suspecting you," I said.

Hal was looking at me with a quizzical expression. "One foul sweep? You mean one fell *swoop*, don't you?"

"No, I think it was pretty foul."

"Doesn't matter what you think, Vic. Like you said, you're just along for the ride. The irony is, even if the virus in you has been eradicated, you're still going to die, anyway. But more quickly, so be thankful for that. The point is, I need to keep my footsteps invisible so nobody can follow us where we're going. That's all that matters. It's the destination that counts in this case, Vic. Not the journey, or the detours. Or even the passengers."

I tried to think, but it was difficult to focus. My guess was when Brett took off after the cowboys, he didn't remain in pursuit, but headed back to the house to take out everyone there. And then blame it on the cowboys, per Hal, who had just privately copped to mass murder without even blinking an eye. He may as well have been telling me what he had for dinner. It was as cold and calculated as balancing a spreadsheet. Not that I would know anything about that stuff. I can't even balance my checkbook.

Reluctantly I looked over at Brett. He didn't return my gaze, but he didn't seem too happy. Well, he never seemed happy, but now he seemed downright unhappy. Something about his demeanor seemed off all of a sudden. But since he was so subtle when it came to any sort of communication, I couldn't discern the distinction.

Actually, what Hal said made sense, per his own twisted version of logic. I would have a lot more trouble believing David Palmer would order a hit on his own daughter, even if they were estranged. It just didn't add up. But then as I said, I've always sucked at math.

Hal stepped back on the gas and headed toward a hangar in the distance. I didn't talk because I had nothing else to say. Plus Hal was so hair-trigger homicidal that any wrong word from me at this point could result in Brett bashing my nose through the back of my skull, at Hal's directive. So I clammed up until we climbed out of the car and headed for the plane. I've always hated flying because I feared the plane would crash and I would die. Now it seemed like the best possible outcome, under the circumstances, as long as Hal and Brett went down with me.

But before we could actually board the plane, machine gun fire erupted. Some bullets hit the plane's gas tank and it exploded, sending all three of us flying through the air, action-movie-style. Brett took the brunt of it since he was closest to the plane when it blew up, but he shook off any signs of shock or pain, and returned fire with a vengeance. I didn't have a gun so I just lay on the floor and prayed to Sinatra or Elvis or Whomever might be listening that might actually feel sorry for me, and be in a position to help.

The machine gun fire abruptly ended when Brett took out the two shooters that had been hiding in the shadows. I stood up and recognized them as the cowboy hitmen. Hal walked over and spit on their dead bodies.

"I thought they worked for you," I said.

"Change of plans, yet again," Hal said as he watched his plane, and hangar, burn around us. "They'd outlived their usefulness, anyway." His favorite fucking phrase.

Now I wondered: did the cowboys decide to turn on Hal, before he turned on them? Or was someone in Hal's proximity the true target, once again? Meaning me. Or even Brett. Man, I really wanted to figure this shit out before I croaked. But it kept getting more complicated, further delaying a clean resolution to a series that had already been announced as cancelled. Something told me this story—*my* story—was going to end in a very unsatisfactory, ambiguous manner, leaving a lot of lingering, unanswered questions, like the infamous fade-out finale of *The Sopranos*. But then that's how most real life stories end, anyway. If not all of them. Even yours.

Hal led us to a jeep parked just outside the hangar, obviously planted there for an expedient, emergency getaway such as this. "I hope you still have your passport, Vic."

I checked the pocket of my white slacks. No wallet, but I did have my passport. They had supplied the only thing I would need for this one-way trip.

"Where are we going?"

"Different plane, different hangar that David never knew about."

"Nearby?"

"Just across the border."

"You mean in Arkansas?"

"No. Mexico."

Then we sped off in the jeep, the humid Texas night air filling my head like a hot air balloon. If only someone would pop it like a pimple on the ugly face of the Earth.

Chapter Nine
LUCHA MUCHACHA

So this brings us back to where I started: on the way down to Latin America for a rendezvous with Fate, my pimp.

This is where things *really* get weird, so hang on. It's going to be a bumpy ride, even bumpier than our jeep on those dusty Texas backroads across the border. I didn't even need my passport, as it turned out. Hal just waved at some border rangers (well, I assumed, given their guns, attitudes, and sunglasses), and they let us cross over into an extremely remote desert that all looked the same to me. My pal Hal seemed to know everybody. Or more importantly, they knew him.

I had no hat or sunglasses anymore, lost in transit, at least until Brett tossed me a pair of expensive Ray-Bans, identical to mine, but obviously brand new. I didn't say much during the drive. There was nothing to say, really. Laura, Jade and Fifi were dead, and their killer was now my captor. No one would probably ever hear about their deaths, either. My guess was Hal had made some kind of arrangement for their charred corpses, or set it up so it would look like the result of a private meth lab mishap. Only Dianne's death made the papers, since she was the sole casualty of the Texas Tiki Bar Massacre, which was in reality a domestic and/or professional dispute designed to look like yet another random public shooting, while the actual massacre was chalked up to an accident, if it was chalked up at all by anyone. I was one of the few people that knew the whole truth, and soon that would be buried with me, too.

I pondered all of this senseless tragedy, centered around a missing dog, as the monotonous, desolate landscape sped past us, or vice versa. My two separate human bite wounds along with my two separate gunshot wounds still hurt, not to mention my smarting scrotum where Hal had injected me with the first alleged antidote. I still didn't feel any effects of the so-called "virus," so it was hard for me to feel relieved I'd been "cured." I was disturbed about the prospect of Hal feeding me a ham sandwich while I was under hypnosis or whatever, but I didn't really believe him. In fact, he had zero credibility by this point, at least as far as I was concerned. In my present predicament, all I could do was try to stay alive long enough to find and rescue Fido, if he was still alive. I feared I'd never even see my beloved Seattle again, instead rotting someplace near the sunbaked equator, literally Hell on Earth, at least to a hardcore pluviophile like me.

I kept hoping Colonel Glenn Manning, A.K.A. *The Amazing Colossal Man*, would show up, pick up the jeep, dump us out, and eat us, since in the sequel, 1958's *War of the Colossal Beast,* he was hiding out here in Mexico, his face horribly disfigured due to his fall from Hoover Dam in the 1957 original. Of course, he was killed in the finale of the sequel, up in L.A. This was one of those American International Flicks where they made the final few seconds in color, for some reason, even though the rest of the movie had been in glorious black and white. I think I read Sam Arkoff saying it was so the audience would remember the entire movie in color, saving them the cost. They did the same thing with *I Was a Teenage Frankenstein* in 1957, and *How to Make a Monster* in 1958. In my case, my last scene would probably be in black and white, and that's how my colorful life would play as it flashed before my eyes in my final moments.

Of course, neither *The Amazing Colossal Man* nor *War of the Colossal Beast* were actually documentaries, so there was zero chance of a sixty-foot tall atomic giant coming to my rescue. It was fun to imagine it, though.

Previously my only experience in Mexico had been a trip to Acapulco back around the turn of the century, meaning this one, trying to locate a wealthy client's missing daughter, who had disappeared down there while visiting an old college boyfriend. I never found her, I mean not on purpose, and in fact I lied and reported she'd been kidnapped and killed by the Cartel, because she had a drug habit. Of course, I only fabricated this excuse to run through the client's expense account after spending about a week at a seaside resort called Las Brisas, a hillside dotted with cute pink bungalows right on the Bay, seen in the 1967 Dean Martin/Matt Helm movie *The Ambushers*.

Once I was back in San Francisco, I read an article in the *Chronicle* about a missing UC Berkeley student who had apparently leapt to her death off the famous diving cliffs at La Perla Restaurant, where I actually dined on the client's dime a couple of times, because I'd seen it in an Elvis movie, *Fun in Acapulco*. I doubted she was an overly enthusiastic Elvis impersonator, though. Maybe just a really devoted if deluded fan wanting to join The King in the hereafter. Presuming he's actually dead, of course.

Naturally the client, who had been directly informed by authorities of his daughter's demise, was extremely pissed I lied about the Cartel connection, and threatened to sue me. I had no real money to fork over, but I could still lose my P.I. license as a result of a court battle I was sure to lose.

So, figuring it was the cheaper and less risky of my options, I flew all the way back to Acapulco out of my own meager savings, this time traveling on a much less extravagant budget, and dug up dirt on the boyfriend, which I should've done in the first place, except I was having too way much fun in Acapulco, banging the local talent, even though I hated the heat. That's one reason I didn't go out often to look for the missing girl. I tried to remain indoors as much as possible, drinking and screwing. At least during my first trip. Now I was forced to actually work, not just for free, but at my own expense, so my selfish subterfuge backfired on me, as it usually does.

Anyway, after interrogating one of my Latina charges down there, a waitress in the restaurant at Las Brisas who spoke very little English (which worked to my advantage, seduction-wise), it turned out the boyfriend had actually pushed the "suicidal" girl off the cliff, and he actually *was* involved with the Cartel, as one of their United States suppliers/couriers. I was vindicated, and the *Chronicle* updated the story, giving me full credit. The client didn't sue me. He just sent some guys over to beat the shit out of me instead. I guess I deserved it. But I still had a hell of a vacation, in fact two, mostly if not entirely for free. And I didn't care I had cheated and lied. The client was a rich, condescending Silicon Valley asshole and his daughter was a spoiled, stuck-up princess, at least according to her sorority sisters, one of which informed me via pillow talk that the princess really *was* a drug addict after all, and that her boyfriend was also her dealer. The reason he pushed her off the cliff remained a mystery, however, and he turned up dead a few months later, just another victim of the Cartel, or that's how the local authorities figured it. So as far as I was concerned, it all evened out in the end.

I often got lucky that way, solving cases pretty much by accident, getting laid copiously along the way. This is one reason Fate was, and remains, my pimp, even as a dog walker. Not much had changed. Trouble still followed me everywhere, and now it was even dragging me along. It has caught up and surpassed me.

Now my third trip South of the Border, down Mexico way (as Frank sang) was being endured rather than enjoyed, at least so far. It didn't feel like it was going to improve before we hit Costa Rica, either.

Making matters worse, Nick drove to yet another remote desert outpost and we boarded a god damn helicopter. I *hate* those things, and in fact I had never actually been a passenger on one, due to my fear of heights. Planes were bad enough. But with helicopters the distance between you and the ground seemed that much more evident, since you could see everything, without any sexy stewardesses for distraction. I actually threw up about five minutes after we'd been in the air, right on Brett's lap. He hit me once in the jaw, mercifully knocking me out for the duration, though I don't think that was his intention.

We landed somewhere near an Aztec pyramid, which was pretty cool. It was dusk, and I swore I saw Popoca, the Aztec Mummy of Mexican monster movie fame (in my house, anyway), his spooky shadow shambling along the distant, glowing horizon. Maybe I was just hallucinating from dread and dehydration, desperately reaching for some familiar connection with my strange surroundings.

A stretch limo was waiting for us, driven by some pockmarked chauffeur that looked like Sid Haig, right there in the middle of the pyramids, which were silhouetted against the red, yellow and purple sky like mysterious, majestic monoliths on the moon. It was positively surreal. But at least I'd survived the helicopter ride, and the limo had air conditioning and a bar stocked with ready-made margaritas, served on the rocks, not blended like an alcoholic slushy. Herb Alpert and the Tijuana Brass were playing on the sound system, while one of the old Aztec Mummy movies was playing silently on the little drop-down TV screen, which may have been the source of my hallucination. Or else Hal was once again reading my mind. I wasn't sure at the time. Didn't matter. If nothing else, Hal was a helluva host, even if I was being led to my own slaughter via the cinematic scenic route.

"Just trying to keep you comfortable, Vic, as always," Hal said as we toasted. "Like a free-range chicken. At least until we reach our, well, your final destination. Salud."

"Yeah, cheers to that, I guess."

For a moment I almost forgot Hal had ordered the murders, via his zombie henchman Brett, of Laura, Jade, Fifi, and Fake Fido, not to mention the horny homeless dudes, but at this point I decided to dig the fact I was being held captive in classic style. I bet the Cartel's accommodations for prisoners weren't nearly as gracious, so I was doing relatively well, all things considered.

Mexico City was a massive maze of zig-zagging cars, ancient buildings barely standing right next to gleaming high-rises, thousands of people mobbing the haphazard streets, and little dogs running around everywhere. Fido might've been among them, but it would've been impossible to tell. I had no idea why Hal was here, or why he required my company and assistance. I was just enjoying the hell out of my margarita, the movie, and the music. My usual distractions from death.

We finally stopped at an ancient fortress that had been converted to the Boutique Hotel Cortes, right in the seductively dangerous heart of it all. Thunder boomed in the distance and a rainstorm suddenly descended, the dark sky intermittently lit up by lightening, and though it was as muggy as a swamp, the moisture felt good after spending so much time drying up in the merciless desert sun.

The Hotel Cortes was downright eerie, like being trapped inside an ancient, open air temple of demonic worship, with little rooms surrounding a courtyard where several shady looking characters sat around drinking and eating, oblivious to the rain. Hal led me to my own private room on the second level, which was tiny and simply equipped with a bathroom, a rickety bed, and a small TV. My sense was that it had once been utilized as a torture chamber, centuries before its present state of commercialized hospitality.

"Don't drink the water," Hal said simply as he led me

inside. "I'll be back for you in the morning. We'll have breakfast in the courtyard and discuss our next move. It's going to be a big day, so try to get some rest."

"Can I shower at least?"

"Please do. And use soap. Just be careful not to swallow any of it. The water, that is. I need you healthy so I know if you're getting sick from the virus, as opposed to the local plumbing."

After he left, locking the door behind him, I peeked out the window. Brett was standing guard. At least the room had air conditioning, which I put on at full blast, both for the cool air and the white noise.

While taking a giant, wet shit in the scary-looking toilet, fearful something with fangs was going to reach up and bite my ass, I read the hotel brochure. Apparently I was "in the vicinity of The Museum of Fine Arts, Alameda Central and Paseo de la Reforma," located at Av. Hidalgo 85 Colonia Guerrero, Mexico City, Mexico. According to the brochure, this building was built in 1620, confirming my suspicions that horrible things had happened right where I was sitting, and I don't mean Montezuma's revenge. Well, not just that, anyway.

In fact, I had a touch of diarrhea myself, but I attributed that to nerves. I carefully washed my ass as well as my many wounds, and then lay on the creaky bed after turning on the TV. Apparently there was a Mexican version of TCM, and I recognized my three *amigos*, El Santo, Blue Demon, and Mil Mascaras. It was an old favorite of mine, *The Mummies of Guanajuato*. Suddenly I felt better. Well, relatively. Then I looked up and noticed a pair of bats hanging on my wall, near the ceiling.

I jumped up and freaked out, but they remained still. Then I realized I shouldn't alarm them, so I laid back down, just in time for a tarantula to appear at the foot of the bed. I thought maybe I was hallucinating again, but I didn't want to take a chance. I remembered James Bond dealing with the same situation in *Dr. No*, so I just lay there sweating as it crawled up the blanket and onto my body, which was mostly nude except for my boxers. And unlike Sean Connery, there wasn't a plate of glass between the spider and my skin. After sweating it out a bit, I jumped up and beat it to a pulp with my own shoe, just like 007. The bats slept through all of it. I mean, if they were sleeping. It was hard to tell.

Suddenly I felt like drinking a dry Martini—shaken, not stirred. In fact, I had never felt more like James Bond than I did during this case, which really wasn't a case, since I hadn't been hired, just drafted against my will. There was no financial incentive. My only motive was basic survival. But that's how it always is with crappy jobs. After all, I was actually a retired detective. In fact, I wasn't really ever a true "detective" to begin with, which explains my rather questionable work ethic. It was just something I started doing because my freelance writing career dried up, and I had no other marketable job skills. Plus I was literally searching for my long lost love, Rose, who actually wound up finding me. But that's another story.

I fell asleep during the next movie, which was like a Mexican version of *Beach Party* or something, when I was awoken a few hours later by the sensation of someone sucking my cock.

Figuring it was a wet dream, which I didn't want to acknowledge for fear of waking up, I looked down and saw a young girl that looked like Salma Hayek in *From Dusk Till Dawn* (well, at least to me) going down on me, her large, brown breasts and long, jet black hair pouring over my thighs and crotch like premium tequila over ice. She suddenly stopped after making eye contact with me, smiling with some of my semen on her luscious lips, then she kissed her way up my quivering loins and sweaty chesty and then to my groggy face, straddling me as she inserted my throbbing boner into her moist, tight pussy. I came hard once, then as she kissed and rode me some more I came again, and again.

It wasn't until my fourth orgasm that I looked up and noticed one of the bats was missing. Then I passed out from exhaustion and pleasure, not knowing or caring if I was dreaming.

When I woke up, the girl was gone. Sunlight was streaming through the curtain on the little window. The TV was still on, now playing something old and in black and white, set in a nightclub, like a Mexican *film noir*. I stared at it a bit, still smelling the strange, beautiful girl's flesh and fluids and cheap perfume. According to the lingering scents, it hadn't been a dream.

I looked up and noticed both bats were there now, asleep. I felt a sharp pain in my throat, on the other side of the "zombie" bite. I went to the bathroom and looked in the mirror. She had given me one nasty hickey, though it looked more like another bite, but smaller, with two distinct puncture marks.

So if not a zombie, I'd turn into a vampire. It was worth it. I had nothing better to do with my pointless life now. Plus I already hated the sun, so I wouldn't be missing anything, anyway.

I went down to the patio below where Hal and Brett were sitting, eating their complimentary breakfast. I heard the classic 1967 Sinatra/Jobim album being played, one of my very favorites. Even here, Hal was my personal DJ.

"Sleep okay, Vic?" Hal asked me, smiling as usual.

"Yeah, eventually," I said. "Thanks for the human Xanax."

Hal winked at me and slapped me on the shoulder. "Prostitutes are like room service around here. They just put it on your tab. Which I'm picking up, of course."

Prostitute. Damn, I hadn't been wearing protection, but then she literally ambushed me anyway. I came all up inside of her multiple times, in several orifices, which meant I might've infected her with something, like a zombie virus, in case that second antidote was just a placebo, since it was concocted with the blood of Fake Fido, from what I knew. Maybe that was the whole idea. Hal was still experimenting on me. I didn't press the issue. Plus it sure beat another shot in my scrotum.

So I just ate my breakfast in appreciative acquiescence, enjoying the soundtrack, before finally asking, "So where to now?"

"We're going to see a wrestling match," Hal said.

"Really? Like, *luchadores*?"

"Exactamundo."

"Wow. Cool. How come?"

"Why not?"

"Good question. I used to ask just plain 'why' all the time. But 'why not' seems more appropriate for just about everything in life. It's easier not to answer."

"Good philosophy, Vic. I'd say that would take you far, but you don't have far to go at this point. *Vámonos*."

Brett stood and pulled the chair out from under me. Apparently we were in a hurry.

"Seems a little early for a wrestling match," I said.

"It's two o'clock in the afternoon," Hal said. "Matinee show. This was lunch. Not breakfast. I let you sleep in. I figured you needed it."

"Um, thanks," I said, even though his final plan was to put me permanently to sleep, though to his credit, he did seem to adjust his agenda according to circumstances. So I held out hope I might actually live through all of this, even as a zombie or vampire or werewolf or whatever. All three beat being a private eye, that was for damn sure. Inside my head, Sinatra's voice still resonated, except now he was singing, "I'm Gonna Live Till I Die."

Once we were outside the hotel, ready to climb into the waiting limo, a barrage of bullets erupted from nowhere and everywhere. This type of sudden, violent outburst was getting monotonous, even to me. Brett hustled Hal and me into the back as he returned fire, then the pockmarked chauffeur that looked like Sid Haig took off, quickly merging with the chaotic traffic. I didn't hear any sirens, just some more gunfire in the distance, and bullets ricocheting off the impervious glass and body.

"This happens all the time down here," Hal said calmly. "Not just to me, either. Lots of people. For all I know, we weren't even the intended targets. We probably lost them by now, anyway. Easy to do. So many damn cars running inadvertent interference."

"David Palmer's thugs, seeking payback for setting up their boss?"

Hal shrugged. "Who knows? I have enemies everywhere, as you astutely surmised. But I have even more friends everywhere, in much higher places, so no worries. Just relax and have another margarita, Vic. You have time for at least one before we get there."

"There" was a kind of club—apparently a renovated gym or something—on the outskirts of the city, judging by the relatively destitute, deserted neighborhood, without a single structure in sight from this or even the previous century.

Just as we pulled up, my crotch starting itching. I put my right hand down my pants and pulled out a teeny little critter from my pubic hair.

"That hooker gave me crabs," I said to Hal when we got out of the limo.

"The seafood here is the best, Vic!" Hal said with a laugh. "C'mon, we can treat that later. Or rather, you can, right now. Here." He took out a flask and handed it to me. "Just pour that down your trousers. It'll kill 'em all, trust me."

We were standing on the street. Little kids were playing soccer nearby. "You mean here and now?"

"Yes, but save some for a swig. That's part of the

treatment."

"All right, fuck it," I said, since my balls were itching like crazy, and it didn't look any better to walk around in public scratching myself. I poured the ointment down my pants. It burned like hell. But when the pain subsided, so did the itching sensation, as if I'd drenched my dick in acid. As instructed, I drank the rest of it, then immediately spit it out. It tasted like iodine. I mean, it tasted like what I assumed iodine might taste like.

"What the hell is that stuff?" I said as Brett gave me a little push inside the door. My crotch had a big wet stain on it, like I'd pissed myself.

"Ancient Aztec remedy," Hal said. I didn't believe him, of course. "Now c'mon, there's someone I want you to meet."

Once we were inside the makeshift arena, the entire atmosphere changed. It was insufferably crowded and annoyingly noisy, people shouting and cursing and laughing, and in the center of the ring at the middle of the expansive room were two masked wrestlers, engaged in battle. Off in the corner a cockfight was in progress, and in yet another corner, near the bar, people were playing cards. Basically this was just a gambling sports joint, with live entertainment, like a Mexican ghetto casino/speakeasy, since it wasn't even designated with a proper sign, other than a neon knockoff of the Aztec god-monster Quetzalcóatl (which I recognized from the 1982 Larry Cohen flick, *Q*). I guess you just had to know it was here. Or know the right people. Or wrong people, depending on how you defined right and wrong, if at all.

Overall, the place had a very sleazy, grindhouse atmosphere, making me think of one of my favorite Mexican monster movies, 1969's *Night of the Bloody Apes*, which was actually a much more explicit remake of 1964's *Wrestling Women vs. the Aztec Mummy*, both by the same director, René Cardona. Just FYI.

"Okay, you're up next, Vic," Hal said, nodding toward Brett, who took me by the arm and led me toward the ring. I was being thrust into the B movie of my own brain.

"Up for what, karaoke?" I said nervously. "I *hate* that shit."

"Put this on," Hal said, handing me a colorful *lucha* mask. But it wasn't silver, like Santo's. It was red, like Santa's. Then I noticed it was actually a Spider-man mask, but with the eyes cut out so I could actually see. The theme song to the 1960s cartoon, my favorite as a kid, played in my head, and I actually got a little excited. Somehow I doubted it was officially licensed Marvel merchandise. More like a customized, bootlegged Halloween mask.

"Um, *why*?" I had to ask.

Then I looked up and saw a lone masked wrestler standing in the center of the ring, taunting me.

"You gotta be fucking kidding," I said.

Hal laughed. "It's amateur night, Vic, rather, and I volunteered your services! C'mon, you owe me after last night's little match, right? I mean, I missed that one, though Brett told me all about it."

That revelation was shocking for two reasons, but I only openly addressed the second. "Brett can talk?"

"No, he used sign language," Hal said, rather sarcastically, so I wasn't sure of his veracity, as usual.

"You know, it's not even nighttime," I said. "So how can it be amateur *night*? We're too early!"

"This is like Vegas, Vic. No sense of time here. It's midnight around the clock. C'mon, you can't keep 'em waiting. People have put money down on this."

"On me, you mean?"

Hal laughed again. "No one is here to lose their shirts, Vic. Well, except you, maybe. Take it off."

"No!"

Then Brett stuck his gun to my head. I sighed with resignation, dutifully removed my aloha shirt, revealing my pasty, soft but sturdy, middle-aged torso, as well as my crotch-stained white trousers. I really needed to get to a washing machine at some point, or else augment my austere wardrobe. Then I put on the mask and reluctantly climbed into the ring, shaking like a man on a fuzzy tree. The crowd went nuts.

The other wrestler was built like a brick shithouse. Meaning the kind I'd love to put my penis in. She was obviously a woman, very voluptuous, wearing purple tights, a long shiny gold cape, gold gloves, sparkly gold boots, and a gold *lucha* mask. The crowd was chanting her stage name: *La Loba! La Loba! Lo Loba!* It translated to "The Wolf-Woman," just like Rino Di Silvestro's classic 1976 Spanish horror movie *Werewolf Woman* (you've never heard of it, never mind). Didn't matter what they called her. This hour-glass-shaped bombshell was about to kick my ass.

And I let her. Well, okay. I put up something of a fight, strictly for the crowd's benefit, not to mention for the sake of what was left of my own fragile male pride, but the fact is, she was just too strong for me. She kept putting me in all of these fancy holds. I was already sore from my fixed bout the night before, plus I had five different flesh wounds still causing pain, so I was in no shape to wrestle anyone. And on top of everything else, she was a woman, so I wasn't sure where I was allowed to grab her. Certainly not her pussy. I wasn't the Commander-in-Chief, after all. Her tits seemed off limits, too. Perhaps I was being too gentlemanly about this. The truth was I just wanted to get it over with. I feel that way about too many things as I grew older. Now I just wanted to make sure I did grow older.

In less than two minutes she had me pinned. The crowd was cheering for her, while jeering at me. Per tradition, she pulled off my loser's mask, revealing my naked humiliation. Then, still mounting me triumphantly, though it was a hollow victory at best, given my sad state, she took off her mask, too.

I recognized her immediately. It was Esmeralda Ava Margarita Valentina Valdez, the Latina beauty that had promised two and a half decades earlier to sleep with me if Donald Trump ever became president, a confluence of events neither of us thought would ever be possible.

I smiled. She screamed.

Chapter Ten
MEXICAN BEAT-OFF

After everything that had happened so far, saying I was "shocked" to see Esmeralda Ava Margarita Valentina Valdez (or "Val," as I liked to call her, partly because I'm lazy but also because of its similarity to my surname) after all this time, in such an improbable place, under such bizarre circumstances, sounds almost trite. I mean, next to zombies and vampires and shootouts in the streets from Vancouver to Mexico City, all for the sake of finding a missing dog, how could this latest cosmic coincidence possibly impress me?

Well, it did. Out of all the aforementioned outrageous events, this one hit me the hardest. Literally. In fact, she could sense just how hard I felt it when she was sitting on top of me in the middle of that ring, surrounded by her adoring fans. But I was obviously her biggest.

She got up off of me and ran out of the ring toward a back room, and I followed her, with Brett and Hal hot on my heels. Hal did say he had someone he wanted me to meet, which meant he actually knew Val—or maybe he was bullshitting me, hard to tell with that guy—but I was determined to find out.

Val went through the door and slammed it shut and locked it behind her, but I actually kicked it in, charged with adrenalin and lust that had been building for a quarter of a century. I was pretty much ready to burst.

She looked exactly how I'd remembered her in my wet dreams since I'd first laid eyes on her, only better.

By now, she was around my age, or rather a few years

younger, since she was in her early twenties when I first met her, on one of my very first cases, shortly after moving to San Francisco from Brooklyn, only because I had a feeling my true love Rose was now living out there. I was right, as it turned out, much to my ultimate chagrin. But again, that's another love story. A very violent one. At least emotionally speaking. Those are the worst wounds, the ones on the inside that no one else can see, only you can feel, because they never fully heal.

The "case" I was on back then involved, ironically, a missing cat. Val had posted some signs about her lost pussy around the Richmond District, where I was living at the time, in a room above The Drive-Inn. Doc Schlock was my landlord and then he became my confidant and best friend. I was lonely and horny as hell, much more so than now, because I had no release. This was before Monica relieved some of my anxiety, and before I found Rose, or vice versa. I had a lot of trouble hooking up with women after Rose vanished on me in New York, since I felt so completely destroyed, emotionally and egotistically.

So when I saw that sign posted on a pole down the block, I essentially hired myself to find the cat, which I did, initially just to prove to myself I could be a real "detective." It actually showed up on my doorstep, hungry and scared, setting a standard of random case resolutions that became the hallmark of my so-called career, though it's not a *modus operandi* you'd find in the standard private eye handbook.

Once I met the drop-dead gorgeous owner, who indeed told me to drop dead, I figured it was Fate, my pimp, in action, because I was instantly attracted to her in a way I'd never been to any woman, besides Rose. After the cat showed up on my doorstep, like a special delivery from Frank Sinatra, I called the number on the poster and told her I had recovered the cat, she told me where she lived, thanked me in person without inviting me in, paid me, then basically told me to fuck off after I made improper advances, essentially offering to take it out in trade.

The slap in the face she gave me in response, along with the condition she'd only fulfill my proposal if Donald Trump became president, resonated with me ever since, even though I buried it in my subconscious, figuring given the terms for that extremely unlikely prospect, I'd never, ever hook up with her. *Ever.* So I forced myself to forget all about her, and redoubled my efforts to reconnect with Rose. That didn't pan out, and neither did any of my subsequent romances, which is why I basically just settled for a series of sexual liaisons without any strings attached. Flash forward to the November 2016 election, and suddenly it all came back to me. I'd been trying to compensate for that one missed opportunity. And failing miserably.

Now here we were, twenty-five years later, in a Mexico City dive, and I was still chasing down her pussy, and she was still slamming a door in my face.

The main difference now, of course, besides the fact we were both much older, was that Donald Trump actually *was* president. I never thought I'd be grateful for something so detrimental to the rest of the planet. But fuck 'em. Humanity as a whole never did anything for me, anyway. I owed them nothing. They deserved exactly what they got. Me, I deserved my belated reward for finding Val's long lost pussy, whose name was actually Gata—not entirely original, but I didn't realize that till much later, after I'd picked up a little Spanish. Waitress in Acapulco, that is. Even later I discovered that GATA was street slang shorthand for Get After That Ass, which I took as another sign of eventual conquest, at least in my wildest fantasies. This was beyond even those, and that's pretty fucking far out there.

Brett tried to stop me from going through the door, so I did what I should've done a while ago: I turned around and kicked him in the balls. I don't care if you're Superman: a direct hit to the nut sack will temporarily stop any male dead in his tracks. It hurts like fucking hell. I should know. It's been done to me plenty of times, figuratively and otherwise.

Brett bent over in agony, but I had no time to enjoy the sight, since Hal was right behind him. I socked Hal once in the jaw, and he reeled back long enough for me to go through the broken door, which led to a dark little dressing room, which itself led to an alley outside. The back door was open. Val had fled the premises. That's how freaked out she was at the idea of fulfilling her own wiseass contract. Too bad. Time to pay up.

I ran down the alley, still sensing Brett and Hal behind me. Unfortunately, I didn't get too far, since Brett shot me in the calf, the bullet taking a chunk of flesh without any penetration, and I fell. Still, I got right back up and continued my pursuit, hobbling like a, well, zombie.

Val heard the shot, turned around, and actually came back to get me. I noticed she had put her mask back on, for some reason. She pulled up and helped me into her waiting car, a late 1960s model white Jaguar, too cool and hot for words. Like her.

She tossed me into the passenger seat and sped off, with Brett firing at us, but she was too skilled a driver. Her gold cape fluttered in the breeze, like a flying superhero. I wondered what other talents lurked within her wealthy well of exotic expertise.

I was madly, hopelessly, desperately in love for the first time in many a moon. Meaning Fate, my pimp, had been mooning me for twenty-plus years. Now it was time he kissed *my* ass. But first, I wanted to kiss hers. If she'd let me.

Raven had been a very kinky, violent lover, often leaving me dazed and bruised following a sexual session, but then she was channeling a lot of justifiable hostility. I guess I had a type. Also like Val, she was bigger than me, but it didn't bother her. I hoped it didn't bother Val. Maybe as an ass-kicking super-heroine, she didn't dig shorter guys.

I could change many things about myself, but not my size. Well, except for that one part, but that thing had a mind of its own. Right now it was standing at attention, ready to receive orders and charge headlong into the fiery field, despite its battle fatigue.

La Loba didn't seem to notice or care. She drove us to a severely secluded villa in the mountains outside wherever the hell we were. I saw the lights of Mexico City in the distance, so I knew we were in some kind of suburb, but it wasn't anything like Friendswood or Pearland, that was for sure. We were in the middle of a god damn jungle.

The villa was poshly appointed, which surprised me. I guess she was a pretty successful wrestler. Or else Hal put her up. But then she just rescued me from Hal. So maybe they weren't in cahoots, after all. I still worried about her safety. Lately any gal that I knew within Hal's social circles wound up dead. Somehow I wasn't too concerned about her, though. She could obviously take care of herself.

I limped inside, leaning on her powerful arm for support, and plopped down on a sofa, careful not to bleed on it, though I was leaking on the hardwood floor. Without saying anything, she examined the wound, got up and poured some hot water into a bowl, grabbed a towel, then wrapped it just above the wound after sucking out the excess blood, before bandaging it. Then she licked her own bloody lips like a cat that had just devoured the canary.

That's when I noticed a bat clinging to a rafter. Just one bat.

Hm.

Anyway, I tried not to think about that too much. I was too enthralled watching her expertly attend to my latest flesh wound. Once again, it sure beat a shot in the scrotum. At least from Hal. She could kick me in the balls for all I cared. Pain from her would feel like pleasure, at least to a romantic masochist like me.

"Funny meeting you here," I finally said as she

tightened the makeshift tourniquet around my calf, just above the wound. Brett had only been trying to slow me down, not kill me. Otherwise I'd be dead. I'm so glad I wasn't. Unless I was. That would be okay, too.

"I don't know what you're talking about," she lied.

I saw right through her strategy of convenient amnesia. "You don't remember me?"

"Should I?"

"San Francisco. Twenty-five years ago. When I was a private detective and Donald Trump was just a buffoonish tycoon. Well, he still is, but I'm no longer a detective. I walk dogs for a living. I also have a cat. You know. Like Gata. Only his name is Doc."

"You're babbling, obviously delirious," she said coolly, avoiding eye contact. "Lie down and rest. I'll bring you some water. After you've recovered, you can leave."

"But those guys may find me and shoot me again," I said.

"Not my problem."

"Then why am I here?" That eternally rhetorical question again, suitable for all occasions, it seemed.

"I felt responsible. But now my responsibility is finished. I have professional nurse training, in fact that's why I was in San Francisco, on a temporary worker visa, so I felt obligated to treat you. I help people in trouble. It's what I do. But I can't make your trouble my trouble. I have too much of my own."

"Baby, you're just the trouble I need right now. Plus you just confirmed we've met, back in San Francisco."

"I admit I lived there. I don't remember meeting you, though. Sorry."

"You positive about that? I couldn't have changed that much. *You* sure haven't."

She ignored me and began stripping out of her costume, right in front of me. By the time she took off her boots and revealed her perfectly shaped, Elmer Battersquality feet, I'd already cummed a little in my pants. I really needed to get them laundered soon. But at the moment I was under her erotic spell. She stood there hovering over me with feminine authority, like a magnificent dominatrix straight out of an Eric Stanton illustration. Her body was still spectacular, even though she was in her late forties at least, by my estimation. Her breasts weren't that big but they stood out and shot me straight in the libido, like banana-shaped bullets. But instead of climbing on top of me again, as I hoped, she turned around and was greeted by another woman, actually a twenty-something girl, whom I also recognized. It was the same one that was in my bed the previous night at the Hotel Cortes.

I looked up at the ceiling and noticed the single bat was gone now.

Val went over and greeted the girl, who as I said looked like Salma Hayek. I always thought Val strongly resembled Raquel Welch, particularly in the 1967 spy flick *Fathom*, with her long, flowing, reddish-brown hair, sharp cheekbones, almond-shaped eyes, and curvaceous figure. At least she did in my memories of our first meeting, now reinforced by our reintroduction. "Salma" was already naked. They embraced and kissed and I came in my pants again. It seemed like they were putting on a show for me, just to torment me. It was my kind of sexual sadism. But then I'm a romantic masochist, as I already admitted.

"Hal told me you were a hooker," I said suddenly, breaking their concentration, as well as the mood.

"Salma" walked over to me, then stood up on the sofa, her legs on either side of me, and peed on my face. I was too stunned to move. Or maybe too turned on. It didn't matter. I almost opened my mouth, even. But I didn't. I did close my eyes, though.

Val laughed and laughed. "Meet my friend," she said. "Her name is Phantasia. That's also her professional wrestling name."

Phantasia jumped off the sofa and into Val's arms, and they retired to another room. I heard sounds of sensuality and whacked off to them, my third orgasm in less than fifteen minutes. My calf wound still hurt, and it was bleeding through the bandage. It didn't impede my self-pleasuring. Mingling pleasure with pain was part of my professional training. It's how I survived. I also imagined I was in Amando De Ossorio's 1974 jungle she-vampire voodoo-zombie classic *Night of the Sorcerers*. That's the only way it made any sense to me.

Completely spent at last, I looked around the sparsely furnished room. There was a Mondrian painting on one wall, and a portrait of Frida Kahlo on another. A bookshelf contained a lot of leftist political stuff, along with plays and poetry. The furniture was all 1960s Swedish style, very *Mad Men*. Val had excellent tastes. Even in women. I whacked off for a fourth time, aroused by the orgasmic cries of lesbian wrestler vampire ecstasy.

I finally fell asleep with sticky hands, a face full of urine, a bleeding leg, and a big, satisfied smile on my face.

When I woke up it was morning. I saw the two bats hanging above me from the rafter. I also heard Julie London singing "Cry Me a River" on a scratchy old record. I sat up and noticed it was playing on a vintage stereo system. For some reason, it struck a chord deep inside of me.

Once I remembered where I was, and who I was with, an incredible thought occurred to me.

I went over and checked out the collection of 45s stacked beside the player. They all rang a bell inside the belfry of my brain.

Twenty or so years ago, after the Rose case, I began receiving a series of anonymous phone messages, back when I had an answering machine. All the caller ever did was leave recordings of classic standards, obviously on LP or 45. No actual words, no context, no follow-up notes, nothing. I never found out who it was, even when I dialed *69, which always either took me to a disconnected number, or one time, seemingly to Graceland and the Ghost (?) of Elvis Himselvis. Eventually I realized that was part of the prank. None of my theories ever panned out. I hoped it was Rose, seeking absolution or reconciliation, but it wasn't. In my many private conversations with Doc, I referred to my mysterious musical stalker as The Phone Phantom.

Now, once again, totally by chance, I believed that cold case had finally heated back up, boiling over with imminent resolution.

Then I looked around the room and noticed something else that nearly made my soul jump out of my skin: Ivar, the sailor statue. The one that had been haunting ever since I arrived in Seattle a couple of years ago. As I told you already, it kept popping up everywhere, and I keep trying to get rid of it, to no avail. I figured it was of supernatural origin, like The Phone Phantom. Except I'd left Ivar back in Ballard. Had Hal brought him to Houston, and now Mexico, along with my other possessions? For what purpose? Just to fuck with my head? That did seem to be a favorite pastime of his.

I looked back up at the ceiling. The bats were gone. But Val and Phantasia were standing there watching me, both wearing flimsy, see-through silk nightgowns over their phenomenal bodies.

"Nice record collection," I said.

"*Gracias*," Val said. Her Spanish accent was subtle, but sexy.

"Cool statue, too," I said, nodding at Ivar.

"Nice hickey," Phantasia said to me with a sly smirk, making me reflexively touch my neck, where she'd bitten me. Suddenly both it and the zombie bite on the other side began to hurt. I guess I only felt them when I thought about them. Like my broken heart.

Val just nodded without actually acknowledging

anything. "How are you feeling?"

I had completely forgotten about my wounded calf, which felt like so much hamburger meat. "Fine," I lied. But then I remembered what she'd told me the night before, about discharging me from her auspices upon recovery. "I mean, not great. I may need a little more time to, y'know. Heal."

She smiled and nodded. "Let's have some breakfast. That should help restore your strength."

"Sure," I said, walking then consciously limping after them toward the kitchen. Along the way I noticed the TV was on, tuned to the Mexican TCM channel. I recognized the film as *Santo vs. the Vampire Women*. By now Phantasia had changed the music to an old LP by Eydie Gormé y Trio Los Panchos. Everyone had my fucking number. I was Captain Obvious.

Suddenly, I realized I still had no shirt, feeling my own man-boobs self-consciously. Just then Val tossed me a peach-colored *guayabera*. In New York they're often referred to as "Puerto Rican shirts," in Miami "Cuban shirts," and in San Francisco they're called "Filipino shirts." I guess here it was just a plain old Mexican shirt. Then I noticed I had no pants on, either, but only after Phantasia tossed me a brand new pair of white slacks, replacing the old blood-stained pair that now also had a bullet hole in the back left leg. Then I noticed that my *huaraches* had been laid neatly by the sofa. While unconscious they had given my paltry itinerant wardrobe a complete makeover.

"What service!" I said.

"Go take a shower before you put them on," Val said curtly, despite the gesture of hospitality. "You stink of piss and blood and semen. You'll find everything you need in the bathroom over there. After breakfast you can go."

She was still behaving as if we'd never met. I didn't bring up the fact that the bats kept showing up and disappearing, and they were never in the same room at the same time as Val and Phantasia. But I had been longing for a shower, for a long fucking time, so I nodded and went into the bathroom, which was very clean and rather luxurious. It was stocked with a razor and shaving lotion, possibly for their male houseguests/victims, but that stuff might've just been there for the sake of their smoothly glorious gams.

When I had finished, we sat down to a simple but sumptuous feast of shrimp cocktails and fresh fruit, with stacks of warm corn tortillas and pitchers of *micheladas* on the side. So on top of being a feminist leftist Latina bisexual masked wrestler/race car driver/nurse, Val could cook, too. I just couldn't let this one get away again. Even if it would be like Wonder Woman dating Chumpy Walnut.

However, I had to clear up one thing first with Phantasia. "Why did you pee on my face?" I asked her.

"Why did you let me?"

I didn't have an answer right away. I thought about it, but nothing came to me that would make any conventional sense. The conversation died abruptly by its own hand.

I turned my attention back to Val and was about to bring up our first meeting again when I noticed a beautiful Siamese cat. Then I noticed a Russian Blue. Then an orange Tabby. Finally it dawned on me we were living in a virtual cat refuge. She must've had a dozen of them, all lounging around in lazy luxury.

This actually segued smoothly into my true conversational agenda. "So I assume Gata is no longer with us? It has been twenty-five years, and she wasn't a kitten when I found her."

"I have no cat named Gata," Val said. "That would be too obvious, don't you think?"

"Not any more," I said. "So you're really going to play this game?"

But before she could answer, or make up another lie, I noticed the abruptly cold expression on both of their faces. They were looking past me.

I turned around and there were Hal and Brett. Hal was smiling. Brett was holding a gun on us.

"C'mon," Hal said curtly. "We have a plane to catch to San Jose."

"California?" I said.

"No, the one in Costa Rica," Hal said. "And I know the way."

"So you're Dionne now?" I said.

"You mean the guy who sang 'Runaround Sue'?" Hal said.

"No. Not *Dion*. Dionne *Warwick*, idiot. You're the one that made the obvious reference."

"I know, Vic. I'm just messing with you. It's become my favorite pastime. Anyway, no time to catch up now. We have dinner reservations. Esmeralda knows the place. Righty, Ezzy?"

Ezzy, I mean Val, didn't respond. She just sighed, wiped her face with her napkin, then stood up. Phantasia remained seated.

"Yes, indeed I do," she said.

I wondered why she looked so sad and powerless all of a sudden. It didn't suit her.

"Take care of the cats," she said as she kissed Phantasia goodbye.

"She's not going with us?" I said.

"No. She needs to watch the cats," Hal said.

"How nice of you."

Brett walked over and kicked me in the calf, right where he'd shot me. I went down, moaning. He lifted me up over his shoulders and carried me outside to the limo and tossed me in the back like a bag of oranges. Val climbed in beside me, still wearing nothing but the nightgown, though I noticed she had on a purple bikini beneath it. She had put on her snakeskin pumps before leaving the villa, though. Same style Jade wore. I guessed they shopped at the same fancy shoe store.

She also put her *lucha* mask back on. When I asked her why, she said, "To protect me from the sunlight."

I wished I had mine, too. That way I could do whatever a spider can. But too late. This web had already been woven. And I was the fucking Fly.

"Help meeee…"

Chapter Eleven
TROPICAL BLUNDER

Now I felt more like Sean Connery as 007 in the pre-credits sequence of *Goldfinger,* on a mission down in some banana republic, except I wasn't wearing a snazzy tuxedo beneath a scuba diving suit after blowing some shit up. I wasn't even wearing a scuba diving suit, because that would mean I'd have to go scuba diving, and to hell with that. I would never blow anything up, either. Not on purpose, anyway. Except maybe metaphorically. In fact, I'm not even close to being James Bond in any way, shape, or form. So it was quite a stretch of the imagination to make such a grandiose comparison. But I managed. This is how I often got through the day. Any day. But especially this one.

While we were in the back of the limo, the window separating us from the driver came down, and he handed Hal a small sack of herbs, along with some rolling papers. Brett proceeded to fashion cigarettes for us, even though I insisted I never smoked in my life.

"But you're from Seattle, Vic," Hal said. "Pot is in the air there. You can't help but inhale it. All you have to do is breathe."

"So that's marijuana?"

"Oh, no. Well, not exactly. It's something much better. My only special formula. I grow it at my compound down in Costa Rica. You'll love it."

"No," I said.

Brett gripped me by the throat and forced a joint into my gaping mouth, shut my jaw with one hand, then ignited my joint with a lighter in the other. Val seemed to have no problem with any of this. By now she'd removed her mask, since the windows of the limo were tinted as well as bullet-proof. Brett cracked a window so we wouldn't suffocate on the fumes. But it still felt and smelled like a luxurious opium den on wheels.

Martin Denny's Moog version of "Quiet Village" was playing, from somewhere, maybe my own muddled mind, as we smoked the strange weed. I was afflicted with reefer madness in about two minutes, probably due to my inexperience with any sort of drugs other than alcohol and Xanax. And sex.

"Why are you making us smoke this shit?" I asked Hal after a few coughing jags, finally inhaling successfully.

"It will make what comes next much easier," Hal said.

"Which is what?"

"You'll see. Just keep puffing, Vic. Trust me."

"Okay," I said, my eyes watering. Val seemed as cool as ever. Brett was abstaining from any sort of hallucinogenic substance indulgence, as usual. His sense of discipline was downright militaristic. Hal wasn't smoking, either. But I didn't care. I felt good. I didn't even mind when the limo finally stopped at yet another private hangar somewhere in the Mexican sticks, and we were shuttled into a waiting private plane, something else I always try hard to avoid, like *karaoke* nights or valet parking (because it requires tips). But my fear of heights wasn't elevated by the experience. I couldn't stop giggling. Or staring at Val, who remained oddly calm and quiet.

That's when I began babbling to her as we sat together in the rear of the plane, which was small but otherwise entirely first class. Hal was throwing back shots of Scotch, while Brett just sat with his massive arms folded and his eyes closed, but I could tell he wasn't sleeping. More like meditating. I didn't even see the pilot, though I assumed there was one. I was high as the sky even without the wings.

I don't remember exactly what I said, but I think the

gist of it was I had been carrying a tiki torch for her since the last time I'd seen her, and I again reminded her of her promise, even if it had been insincere, made in jest. She still pretended she had no idea what I was talking about. I began to worry maybe she wasn't really Esmeralda after all, but just another of my delusional fantasies made flesh. But no, she'd made an indelible impression. It was definitely, absolutely, unmistakably her, all right. She was older now, of course, but somehow even hotter than my image of her, which had been burned then shelved into the recesses of my brain for two and a half decades.

I even told her I had no problem with the fact she was sleeping with another woman, depending on its contract of exclusivity, of course.

"But you like guys too, right?" I prodded her.

"Even if I do, that's not going to help you," she said, finally responding to my blather.

"You don't find me attractive?"

"I'm not even searching."

"So I'm not your type."

"I don't have a type, beyond organic, orgasmic chemistry." I dug her way with words. I dug everything about her. I was entranced, enchanted, and energized for the first time in a long, long, long time.

"So that means you don't necessarily prefer pussies over penises," I said, fingers crossed.

"No, but I'm not into pussies *with* penises, which is too bad for you." She actually made herself laugh. I was getting to her. Or maybe it was the joint. Didn't matter. The ice between us was melting quicker than the Arctic Circle.

"You know, my best friend Monica is bi-sexual," I said, scrambling for common ground while providing proof of my open-mindedness. "She's living with a woman now, in fact. We used to fuck all the time. She goes both ways without even thinking about it."

"Doesn't it seem odd to you that so many women you

sleep with are bi-sexual?"

"I assume they're just reacting directly to sex with me."

"That doesn't sound like a ringing endorsement of your performance skills."

"Maybe I just ruined them for any other man."

"More likely you ruined the whole idea of men."

"You know, insulting a stranger is often an indication of misdirected sexual tension."

"It's also a sign of sincere disdain."

"But you have no reason to hate me."

"Not yet, but the more you talk, the less I like you."

"So I should just up now."

"Please."

I then proceeded to tell her the story of my life. I began with my birth in Brooklyn over half a century ago, continuing in CliffsNotes-style right up until the recent attacks by zombie hoboes in Minneapolis and my raging gun battles with cowboys in Houston, or at least my proximity to them. I'd been caught in the crossfire, anyway, which itself succinctly summed up the story of my life. By the time I was finished, Hal announced were about to descend into San Jose, on his own private runway, of course.

Val didn't seem all that impressed with my abridged autobiography conveyed via live audiobook. I felt like I'd been waiting to tell her about my life for most of my life, since it all seemed to be leading up to this moment, sitting with her on a plane to Costa Rica.

"You're telling your version of your story, but that doesn't mean it's true," she said after I finally finished. She seemed relieved. "Everyone has their own version of the truth. That's why this world is so fucked up."

"You mean like 'Rashomon'?"

"A perverted version, yes. At least in your case. You see the world through your own lens, and your life as a movie."

"People keep telling me that. And I agree. It's the only way I can endure it."

"I understand. But make sure you're not deluding yourself along with everyone else. Then you're just part of the problem. As long as you know the distinction between fantasy and reality, cling to any explanation that makes sense to you, as long as you only realize it's simply a theory, or one potential version of the authentic truth. We all have our own individual ways of looking at this life, informed by our own experiences. No perspective is definitive. But in your case, the truth is perhaps exaggerated more than usual."

"Man, you're deep."

"You have no idea."

"I'd like to find out."

"Forget it."

"Never."

"Too bad for. you."

"You're a co-star in my movie now, so you can't forget me, either. As much as you may want to. You're my new leading lady, in fact."

"Believe me, this is just a cameo."

"But I don't believe you."

"Doesn't mean it's not true."

"People keep saying that to me, too."

"Because that actually is true. You should start listening to people more often, instead of just the voices inside your own head. Then you'd see things for how they really are, instead of how you'd like them to be."

"I try, at least in the moment, but in retrospect, whenever I relate something that happened to me, I may or may not be embellishing it with a cinematic flourish. I've seen so many movies that I can't help but reinterpret or re-envision or re-imagine or recollect or whatever-the-fuck reality via my own personalized B movie prism. It's how I cope with stuff I don't understand. Which is practically everything."

"That's probably why I can read you like a book."

"Well, my life *is* an open book."

"So anyone, say, reading your story may be led to believe things that didn't actually occur?"

"Oh, they occurred all right. Just maybe not exactly as I'm depicting them. You, for instance. Are you even real?"

She looked at me and said, "You'll find out if I'm lying next to you when you wake up."

I nodded and smiled. I was getting through to her, after all. Or so I chose to believe out of sheer desperation.

Then we landed, at last. I was already on the downslope of my high, but at least my flying anxiety had been effectively quashed for the duration of the trip. Brett was probably grateful I hadn't vomited on him again. For my jaw's sake, so was I.

"Do you have any idea where we're headed?" I asked Val as we rose to exit the plane.

"Yes," she said. "It's the nightclub where Hal and I first met. I was working there as a dancer, before I became a wrestler. Many years ago."

"Why are we going there now?"

"Dinner," she said.

"We could eat that anywhere," I said.

"Not this cuisine."

"You think I'll like it?"

"No."

"Can't wait."

Instead of a limo, Brett and Hal led us to a waiting jeep, like the one we used for our Texas road trip, not my fondest memory. But the air was actually a little cooler than I anticipated here in San Jose, and the sun was already setting. I still felt relaxed, but the nagging sense that I was being politely escorted to my doom was beginning to brutally butcher my buzz.

Brett drove us to a really charming, cozy little place

called Melrost Airport Bed and Breakfast, in the San Jose suburb of Alajeula, or so I figured out later. Hal was apparently best friends with the owners, a friendly husband and wife team, who led us to our quaint rooms. Unfortunately, I was bunking with Brett, and Hal was shacking up with Val. When I realized this, my mind was immediately cleared of any intoxicating elements ,and I became downright agitated, then quietly enraged.

Naturally, nobody was interested in my views concerning absolutely anything, so Brett forced me into our room while I watched Val passively following Hal to their room, most likely for a furious fuck-fiesta. That wouldn't be happening in our room. I hoped.

Since I had no luggage, just the clothes on my back (and legs), I had nothing to unpack, even. I just sat on my bed and sulked after turning on the overhead fan, since there wasn't even any air conditioning. I felt like the iron bars of my Second World prison hellhole had just slammed shut, and I was trapped with my intimidating cellmate, indefinitely.

Brett just sat on his own bed, reached into his neatly but fully packed traveling bag, and pulled out a notebook, in which he began to write.

"What are you writing?" I asked, not expecting an answer from this mute bastard, expect maybe in sign language, and he probably only had two words via one finger to offer in reply.

"Poems," he muttered instead, without looking at me.

I was so stunned I didn't say anything for a few moments. Then I said, "So…you *can* talk."

"Of course."

"Then why don't you?"

Brett looked up without meeting my eyes, and said pensively, "Everything I have to say I just write down. I have no interest in conversations unless they're about something of artistic interest to me. You're just business. I don't talk shop, and I don't write during work hours. When I'm on duty, I put aside my notebook, sometimes for weeks at a time, but I'm always thinking, so that when I'm ready to write again, I actually have something to say worth recording."

Then he just continued writing.

"I never met a mass murderer that wrote poetry," I said, immediately regretting it, since he was pretty buff for a literary type.

"Then I guess you haven't met many mass murderers," Brett said, still focused on the page.

"Just you," I said tentatively.

Then he looked directly at me and said quite calmly, "I never killed anyone unless I was defending Hal. That's my job. It's what funds my primary purpose, which is to build a colony for writers and host retreats for writers from all over the world. That's my only goal in life. The rest is just a means to an end."

Again, I had difficulty responding right away, since not only did Brett fully possess the power of language, in both spoken and written forms, but he had a lot more going on in that thick skull of his than I ever imagined.

"So Jade, Laura, Fifi, the bums. They don't count."

"I didn't kill them," Brett said flatly, looking back down at his notebook. "I just found them that way."

"But Hal said he had you kill them."

"He lied. I suppose for your benefit. Or maybe to get a rise out of me. It was a test, which he does often, with me and everyone, to see where we stand on any given issue, and which I always pass because I always ignore it. But the fact is, they were all killed by the same gunmen that hit the bar. And they were hired by Hal. He wanted all the girls taken out, including Dianne. His confession to you about those three was just another way to keep you off your feet. He's toying with you."

"And you let him?"

144

"I don't *let* him do anything. I work for him, not the other way around. Once I reach my financial goals, I'm done, and this will all be behind me. Now shut the fuck up. I'm writing."

"So when did you start writing?" I asked.

He glared at me and it seemed like he was going to actually get up and clobber me, but he took a deep breath, closed his eyes to center his focus, then opened them and said, "When I first had my heart broken, at age twelve. I've been in love many times since then, and it always ended badly. It always does, without fail. Even Jade."

"Jade? You mean you two were an item?"

"For a while, yeah."

"Is that why you felt entitled to rape her?"

He glared at me again, then softened his intense gaze and said, "I didn't rape her. She wanted it. It was that or death, so she chose sex. I was merely prolonging the inevitable by going along with Hal's so-called experiment. He's really just a perverted voyeur, in case you haven't figured that out yet. But then so are you."

"If it was voluntary, then why was she strapped to a table?"

"Like I said, Hal wanted to just off her, but then I suggested we use her as a test subject instead."

"You could've just bitten her."

"No, *you* are the test subject for bites. This was a test for infection from organic semen injection. Would you rather have had me fuck you up the ass? Definitely wasn't my preference."

"Okay, never mind. You did it to save Jade's life, or at least put off the inevitable, because you loved her."

"Yeah."

"But by that point, you'd broken up?"

"Yes. Not my idea, though. I wanted her back. I thought maybe this would change her mind. But then Hal made the call, anyway, so it's too late."

"So it really ended when she died?"

"No. When she left me. I was the one that died first. *Here*. Inside. Where it counts. She was my lifeline. I was dead before I met her, and now I'm dead again."

I was somewhat moved by this confession, if only because I could relate. Naturally I didn't mention the fact she'd seduced me, allegedly in the line of duty. Also, it doesn't take much to seduce me. Anyway, I didn't think he'd take it too well, so I saw no reason to bring it up. "So it was pretty serious between you two, huh?"

"Yes. We were engaged to be married when she changed her mind and left me for another woman, or so she said at the time. Several, in fact. But that wasn't the real reason, I found out later."

Deception was our mutual enemy. "I know how that feels, man."

"No, you don't. You never loved anyone liked I loved Jade."

"Yes, I have. Many times. Once in particular. And I think maybe twice now."

"You mean Esmeralda?"

"Yeah, I guess it's obvious, then. Though I call her Val."

"Her name is Esmeralda."

"One of many names."

"One of many faces," he added cryptically.

"What does that mean?"

"If you don't know already, you'll find out soon enough. If you last that long."

"Okay, what does *that* mean?"

He looked at me for a beat, closed his eyes again as he regained control over his own fists, and said, "For the last time, shut the fuck up until I say otherwise. This is my only time to write. I need it. The whole world needs me to do this, trust me. Otherwise I will go on a heartbroken rampage the likes of which this civilization has never seen."

That's when I decided to shut the fuck up. I lay back on my bed and thought about what he'd told me. At first I thought Jade was wary of seeing Brett back at Psycho Suzi's because it would counteract her power play, given Hal's bodyguard could beat the shit out of hers without breaking a single bead of sweat. But now it seemed it was more due to emotional discomfort brought on by a painful breakup, which she apparently instigated, and she wanted to sidestep any confrontation that may reopen old wounds, at least Brett's, or create new ones, of the physical variety. Poor bastard. Suddenly I felt empathy for my brother in romantic tragedy. Not enough to hug him or anything. I kept it to myself, but I figured it was a card I might be able to play at a crucial moment in this unpredictable and increasingly dangerous game.

A broken heart was most likely the cause of his solemnity, I deduced, rightly or wrongly. Not anger or hate. Just grief. So that's how it was. That's how it always was, or at least much of the time. Everyone is looking for love, but hardly anyone ever finds it, and when they do, it damn near kills them if they can't claim it, or when they lose it. This is why love stories are too violent for me.

Still wide awake, I shut my eyes and dreamed of better days, none of which were behind or directly in front of me, but hopefully on the horizon somewhere ahead, obscured by the mists of my own mind.

La Casa de la Gata was a nightclub somewhere in San Jose, don't ask me where, because I was completely disoriented. I'd never planned on being in Costa Rica, and in fact if you'd asked me to point it out on a map before then, I probably couldn't. For all I knew it was an island in the Caribbean. But it wasn't. It was in Central America between Nicaragua and Panama, which still sounds surreal just writing it here. I felt like I was on an episode of *Miami Vice,* on an undercover assignment, drug dealers everywhere. Only part of that was actually true.

The irony of the nightclub's name didn't escape me. "Gata," I said to Val as we got out of the limo. "Where have I heard that before?" She didn't respond, but she didn't have to. All the pieces were slowly falling into place. However, I wasn't sure I even wanted to see the completed picture at this point. None of it seemed very promising, at least in my regard.

We walked beneath the blazing red neon sign shaped like a jungle cat and into the club, which was bigger than it appeared from the outside, and pleasingly old school, like one of those classy joints in one of those old Mexican *noir* films. It had burgundy-colored curtains and plush black booths lining the walls, with velvet paintings of naked native women and jaguars here and there, and a stage facing the front door. A bosomy babe was about to remove her G-string, and I felt like I was in the right place at the right time. Some kind of vintage bongo music was playing from somewhere, but again, I could no longer distinguish between the jukebox in my head and any exterior sources, so you'll just have to take my word for it.

A *maître d'* escorted us to a booth in the back, near the stage, so I got a good view of the babe, who looked more American than Latin. In fact, she had reddish-blonde hair and very white skin. And breasts the size of watermelons, but with the firmness of coconuts. They looked all real, too.

"God, look at those tits!" I observed with enthusiastic admiration as we sat down.

Hal actually reached over and smacked me on the side of the head. "That's my sister-in-law, Vic, so watch it."

"Your *what*?"

"You heard me. Her name is Molly and she has three kids back in Minnesota. Her husband, my brother, Curt, is sitting right over there. This is her chance to unwind from her stifling Midwestern existence. She's on vacation from being a full-time wife and mother, literally letting her hair down. So show a little god damn respect, you heathen."

A nice-looking older guy with glasses looked over and toasted us with his tumbler of booze. He was sitting ringside, alone, watching his wife drive the crowd wild.

"So she's not your stepsister, at least," I said. Hal ignored me and ordered some food and drinks from the waitress, who was young and sexy, as they always seem to be. I couldn't take any more physical stimulation. I might explode and cover the room in backed-up semen and other disgusting bodily fluids. I felt like a bottle of Coke being shook by a spastic speed freak. Pop that cap and everyone gets wet and sticky. I did my best to hold it in.

Brett had turned his mute button back on, and just stood there silently observing the crowd, seemingly scanning it for any signs of distress or disruption. Val was also quiet, almost bored, actually. Or pretending to be. I couldn't trust any of these poker faces anymore. I decided to strike up a conversation because the silence was just making me more nervous.

"So you've been setting me up for all this for a long time," I said to Hal.

"Life is a set-up, Vic. It's all an illusion. The trick is getting ahead of things by creating your own version of reality."

"How do I know when you're fucking with me, and when you're not?"

"Does it matter?"

"Does anything?"

Hal inadvertently threw my own philosophy right back in my face. "That's my whole point, Vic. Maybe you're the only one that's real among us, and we're just phantoms in your epic dream. Think about it. None of this is actually happening, so none of it ultimately matters. So-called corporeal reality can change in an instant. Watch."

With that, Hal picked up a steak knife, grabbed a passing waiter, and slit his throat, careful not to let any blood splatter on his silky shirt. Instantly two goons, along with Brett, picked up the dead body and carried it out of sight.

None of the patrons seemed to notice. A young poet from San Francisco named Zeke, whom I recognized from some cafes up there, was in the middle of a dynamic performance piece, and everyone was riveted. He was that good.

I pretended not to be fazed by Hal's sudden, casually murderous outburst. No one else at the table seemed particularly bothered by it, either. "Gone," Hal said, snapping his fingers. "That's this ephemeral existence in a nutshell. Now you're here, now you're not. It renders everything ultimately meaningless. This is why I decided to take charge of my own dream, Vic. Because to me, I'm the only real player, and you're all just guests that don't actually exist, unless I allow it."

I nodded my head as if any of that made sense. I noticed Val had rolled her eyes in the middle of that spiel. I guess she'd heard all about Hal's God Complex before. I just hoped that's all he'd shared with her, intimacy-wise.

I shook my head sadly and looked back up at the stage. Molly had returned, wearing nothing but waist and ankle bracelets, doing a kinky belly dance behind Zeke, who continued to riff and rant. Then I noticed a piano player, very distinguished looking, was tinkling the keys in a jazzy mode as accompaniment to the poetry reading, which was getting wilder by the second. Further examination revealed that the piano player was being blown beneath his stool. Meaning piano stool. Midway through the performance the person blowing him stood up and drank some water from a glass on top of the piano, I guess to wash down the semen he'd just swallowed. He looked like he was one of the locals, a beefy young stud wearing nothing but a T-shirt, shorts, and sandals. Then the guy went back to blowing the piano player, who didn't miss a key. It was an incredible display of raw talent from all concerned. They even got a standing ovation when it was over, including from me. The accolades were well-deserved, in my humble critical estimation.

Zeke thanked Molly and the penis, I mean pianist, whose name was Tim, who then publicly acknowledged the contributions of his own musical muse, whose name was Roy. Then I noticed Roy go back to the front door. He was the god damn bouncer. Tim took a break at the bar, and Molly sat down with her husband Curt. They began making out and I got a tremendous boner, since he was sucking on those tits voraciously, and I was right there with him, vicariously. I was practically salivating. I noticed Val just shaking her head, ashamed of her immediate company.

Then another guy who seemed vaguely familiar to me took the mike from Zeke, and introduced himself as Carl Sloane, an expatriate actor now living in Costa Rica, and debuting his new cabaret act. I'd seen him in many movies before, so I was a little starstruck. Tim the piano player hopped back up on stage with his drink, but Roy remained at the door this time. Molly also climbed back on stage to dance completely nude behind Carl, who broke into a jazzy version of the Simple Minds tune, "Don't You (Forget About Me)." How the hell could I, after a spectacle like that? This was my kind of Breakfast Club, served all day long.

I looked at Hal and asked, "So are all clubs in Costa Rica like this?" I said.

"There's no other club in the world like this," Hal said.

"If I'm just a guest in your dream, I guess I could do worse."

"Be patient, Vic. You will."

That crack certainly didn't make me feel any better. "Excuse me," I said. "Where's the bathroom?"

"Brett will take you."

"Really, I can handle this myself, thanks."

"You're a flight risk Vic. Plus I can't take the chance of you missing what happens next."

"I don't know if you can top this act," I said.

"Oh, trust me. This is just the warm-up."

"I'm not fucking wrestling anyone again." That actually elicited a little laugh out of Val, who then immediately resumed her poker face.

"Don't worry, Vic. Go with Brett, and come right back. The real show is starting soon, so make it snappy."

That didn't make me feel any better, either.

Brett led me to the bathroom and stood guard while I went in and peed. Inside was another man, maybe in his forties, tall, wearing fashionable glasses and a stylish white suit. He was sitting on the floor, sobbing.

"What's wrong?" I asked him.

"My boyfriend is an asshole," he said.

"Okay, sorry," I said, going to take a leak, making sure he didn't see my cock as I pulled it out in front of the stall. I doubted he was interested, though. He had a thick, Southern drawl, making me wonder how the hell he got all the way down here. He probably wondered the same thing about me, if he thought about me at all.

So once I zipped up, I asked him.

Turned out he was on the lam from the law. His aforementioned boyfriend was a drug dealer, who got busted during a raid at some party he was hosting. So the boyfriend brought him down here, more or less against his will, to escape the cops up in Atlanta, where they were both from. Now apparently the boyfriend, who got busted anyway, but by local authorities, was in a Costa Rican prison, rotting away, and Justin (he eventually told me his name) was left all alone in a strange country. I felt a bond with him, and sat down next to him, to offer comfort to my lost brother. But then Brett burst into the bathroom, lifted me up, and carried me outside.

That's when I heard the screaming. The screaming

outside my own head, that is.

The entire club had erupted into utter mayhem. Everyone was attacking everyone else, zombie-style. Hal had obviously spiked the food or the drinks or something. At least the food and drink consumed by the paying patrons. Roy was busy beating crazed heads in with a bat, and Brett joined him, only Brett used his brass knuckles, pounding the foaming faces into mush. The two goons that had carried out the dead waiter were also busy fighting off the undead hordes. On stage, Carl Sloane kept singing, Molly kept dancing, and Tim kept playing the piano. I saw Zeke in a corner, jotting down notes furiously, obviously trying to capture the moment in literary form. Everyone has their own coping/defense mechanisms, I guess. Even Carl Sloane kept scratching his nostrils for some reason, which seemed obvious, at least to me. They all appeared completely disconnected from the reality of the situation, except for the few patrons not infected with the foodborne virus. They were simply more expendable subjects of Hal's latest "experiment."

Then I noticed Val had put on her *lucha* mask and was actually wrestling some of the zombified patrons to the ground, kicking others in the head and incapacitating them. Hal just sat back and laughed.

Me, I wondered what the hell he had put in that joint. The one I smoked, that is.

Chapter Twelve
THE ROT PACK

The next thing I knew I was at a remote location called Cascada Pavone, which looked like the cover of a Martin Denny album: a waterfall, stream and natural swimming pool deep in the Costa Rican jungle. All that was missing was model Sandy Warner busting out of a skimpy sarong. Tim the piano player was lying beneath the waterfall, laughing, then Roy popped his head up out of the water, telling me all I needed to know about that situation. Molly was gloriously topless as she frolicked in the water with her equally nude husband, Curt. Zeke was sitting on a rock in the middle of a stream, reciting poetry to no one in particular, apparently right off the top of his head. Carl Sloane was lying on his back, floating in the pool with a blissful, oblivious expression on his face, though his nose was still itchy, apparently, since he kept sniffling. Maybe it was due to allergies, or a cold. Somehow I doubted it.

I looked around further, soaking in the tranquil scene. Even Justin was there, with a Filipino looking dude whom Justin met while fleeing the melee back at Casa de la Gata. The two happy men were passionately kissing and embracing beneath the waterfall, next to Roy, who was holding Tim's head under water as white foam bubbled to the surface. It was about time they switched positions. Only fair.

Brett was standing guard as Hal sat and watched, taking pictures of everyone, like a tourist. I looked down and noticed I was both wet and nude, and so was Val, lying next to me, gazing at me with adoring eyes. She was my own personal Sandy Warner.

"That was wonderful," she said.

"What was?"

She hit me playfully. "Worth the wait," she added. "Maybe we can do it again sometime."

"Do what?"

She gave me a stern look, then laughed. "I know that was the lay of your lifetime, Vic. I never heard a grown man make those kinds of sounds when he came. And you came more often than any woman I've ever been with."

I wasn't sure how to take that, but then I wasn't sure how to take anything. I just went with it. Whether I was trapped in my dream or someone else's, I liked it. Much better than the last one, anyway.

So this was my life now. Going from dream to dream, not knowing who was in charge of it, whose head I was lost in. Maybe it was my own. Perhaps this was the secret of Life. Hal was right. None of it mattered. Just enjoy it before it all evaporates into nothing. And this was definitely better than nothing.

I only wished I could remember having sex with Val, which is what she was obviously referencing. Hopefully it would come back to me. She made it sound so good. If I couldn't recall what was surely my best memory, then maybe this was Hell, after all. I'd find out soon enough. Meantime, I was suddenly hungry. My stomach was grumbling. And fortunately, I wasn't craving brains.

Next we were taken via some sort of tour bus, with air conditioning, to another spot, an open air tiki-type bar called the Villa Leanor at Ballena Beach Club, right near a very quiet, unpopulated stretch of scenic shore in a Pacific coastal section of Costa Rica. Apparently we were in most people's idea of Paradise. All I knew was it was too damn hot, but I tried to ignore that as I enjoyed our drinks and meal and company. The owner was an American expatriate, and had lived around there for years. He was very friendly, and the food and drinks were excellent. It was amazing how sharp my senses were, even in this ongoing dream state.

Afterwards we all went skinny dipping in the ocean as the sun set. It looked like the most majestic painting ever created, and it was painted anew on a nightly basis. Magical. But still, too fucking hot, even at night.

Afterwards we wound up at a fancy seaside resort called El Castillo, which really did look like a drug kingpin's hideout in *Miami Vice*, or the private residence of a Bond villain. We ate and drank and then Val and I swam nude in the crystal blue pool, that seemed to blend seamlessly into the aqua-green horizon. Hal was still documenting everything with his camera phone. I didn't have a Facebook page or I would've told him to upload the photos and tag me. I wanted the whole world to know how happy I was. This was my idea of heaven. Except for the fucking humid night air and god damn bugs everywhere.

Then, like drunken dorks attending a clown convention, we all climbed back into the tour bus, giggling giddily. The driver—once again the pockmarked guy that looked like Sid Haig—took us over a steep mountain forest pass called Empalme Cerro De La Muerte, enshrouded in thick mists, ensconced in foreboding atmosphere. It felt like I was back in the Pacific Northwest, the complete opposite of the steamy, sticky landscape far below our current altitude. I couldn't have dreamed it any better.

The road was long and winding and very dark and I could hardly see anything outside of the bus window, because of the thick fog as well as the nocturnal shroud. I couldn't believe this was still Costa Rica. Hal explained that this road was famous for all the fatal car accidents, hence the name, which translated to "Mountain of Death" or "Summit of Death." He even pointed out a few abandoned wrecks on the wayside. Suddenly, I sobered up. Nobody else did, though. Everyone was laughing while passing around a bottle of tequila that was quickly emptied, till Brett popped open another one. I just sat in silence. Suddenly it all felt very ominous, like we were crossing the River Styx, and I grew uneasy. Val was sound asleep. I put my head on her shoulder and pretended I was also asleep in my own dream. Or maybe hers.

By dawn, we wound up in a dusty little town somewhere called Palmar Norte, in South Puntarenas, wherever the fuck all of that was. (I was only able to pinpoint the whereabouts later, mostly for your benefit, because I wanted to be very specific, so you wouldn't think I was just making all this shit up.) We were in the middle of nowhere, basically. Everyone had fallen asleep by then. The town looked sleepy, too. And deserted, except for a few locals giving us a wary eye. I felt immediately threatened, since I was one of the few gringo interlopers in an otherwise isolated Costa Rican community, far off the beaten path, most likely not found on any tourist maps. I wanted to wake up now. But I already tried that. It never worked anymore.

I noticed a few people stumbling around like zombies. Because they *were* zombies. At least reasonable facsimiles of the walking dead. I disregarded them since they posed no immediate threat, and I was hungry and thirsty.

We went inside and I sat at the bar and put my head down, sobbing from sheer exhaustion and relentless disorientation. The friendly female bartender offered me a beer, which I accepted, apparently on the house. I had one, then another, then another. I couldn't stop crying. Val was still asleep on the bus, I assumed. I just wanted to sit there until I regained consciousness of the real world, or at least some alternative reality to the present one, which just wasn't working for me anymore.

Finally my brain grew woozy, I assumed because it was swimming in all that *cerveza,* and my skull slammed down hard on the bar. When I lifted my heavy head after some indeterminable passage of time, everyone was gone. *Everyone*. Even the bus. I was suddenly stranded in a remote Costa Rican town, entirely alone.

I wandered outside, dodging zombies, looking for someone, anyone that wasn't dead or undead. I called Val's name, to no avail. It was hot as hell, and the rotting flesh of the zombies began to stink up the atmosphere. Ground fog was obscuring my vision, but it seemed way too warm for mist, unlike that eerie mountain passage. Then I realized it wasn't fog, but smoke. There were fires burning everywhere. The citizens had gone insane, burning their own town to the ground, probably accidentally knocking over inflammatory objects, or something like that. The ambience was surrealistic. I felt like I was lost in a Lucio Fulci movie. My life had finally turned into one of the B movies I loved so much. Now I just wanted the final credits to roll so I could go home. No dice.

No matter where I went, up dirty alleys, inside and out of little stores, down the desolate streets, I couldn't escape the infected townspeople. Apparently by now everyone was a victim of the virus, from either infected food or bites, I reckoned, and they'd run out of non-infected people to attack. Suddenly I wish I hadn't been injected with that so-called antidote, so I could just blend in with the crowd. But if the antidote worked, why was I still suffering blackouts and time lapses and delusions, like this one? Maybe the antidote didn't work after all. Or it wasn't an actual antidote, but another version of the virus. At least I wasn't a red-eyed freak frothing at the mouth like these creepy motherfuckers.

I kept running and hiding and fighting off zombies until I was outside the town and deep in the surrounding jungle. I wasn't much better off. There I encountered snakes and spiders and scorpions, or variations thereof, both on land and in the sundry streams, where I waded up to my waist, headed nowhere in particular. A crocodile tried to attack me, but I out-swam it. And I knew for sure it was a crocodile, not an alligator. Alligators have broad snouts, and their teeth jut over their upper haw. Crocodiles have narrow snouts, and their teeth jut over their lower jar. I read that fact in one of my many animals books as a kid.

Monkeys and parrots sang and danced in the trees above me, as if mocking my panic. I was always into tiki culture, but strictly the indoor, *faux*-tropical kind, sitting in a dark, air conditioned bar, drinking cocktails. This was all a bit too authentically exotic for my delicate, urbanized sensibilities.

Then I heard shouting behind me. Human voices. For once, I was glad to hear the sounds of my own fucked-up kind. I fell face-first into a stream, and hoped I'd drown so I could finally wake up from this epic nightmare. I passed out, or maybe I was drowning. I didn't care. I just wanted to be unconscious. Maybe forever. Again, no dice.

When I did wake up, or so I thought, Val and I were lying on another beach, which I later learned was named Playa Ventanas, in Bahia Ballena, surrounded by locals and tourists. There were toucans in the palm trees lining the sand. People were taking pictures of them. Nobody else from the bus was there, not even Hal and Brett. We were finally alone, and seemingly safe in a tranquil environment.

"Where are we?" I asked her.

"Heaven, my love," she said, and then she kissed me, and I didn't care. All was well.

Until the toucans suddenly began exploding, freaking out the tourists. I grabbed Val's hand and we ran back into the god damn jungle, where we encountered more zombies and crocodiles and exploding toucans, so we just kept running and running and running until…

I woke up again. This time I was back in my bed at Melrost Airport Bed and Breakfast in Alajeula. No one else was around. I was almost afraid to get up and see the outside world. Maybe I should just go back asleep and stay that way, I thought. But I was too curious. Then I looked up at the ceiling, checking for bats, but saw none.

Outside on the patio, complimentary breakfast was being served. I saw Hal, Brett, and Val sitting at a table together. Tentatively I joined them, without saying anything.

"Sleep okay, Vic?" I said.

"Never better," I lied, not even sure I had been asleep, or awake.

Val, I mean Hal, handed me a camera, and told me to scroll through the photo roll. There was visually preserved evidence of all of my recent exploits—from the nightclub zombie attack to the waterfall to the beach to the misty mountains to the spooky little town and back to the other beach—including all the craziness I had chalked up to dreams or hallucinations. It all happened. I just couldn't connect them all chronologically, or even logically, since there were two many gaps in my consciousness. It all seemed like a Jess Franco movie: incoherent, but mesmerizing.

"We were hiding on the bus, but keeping tabs on you," Hal said. "Interesting the infected still wanted to bite you and make you one of their own, even though you still have the virus."

"But you gave me the antidote."

"It's not one hundred percent effective. Yet. You're still delusional, but also vulnerable to hypnotic mind control, which is the whole point. Basically you're still under the influence of my opioids, Vic. You're just not cannibalistic, which is an important step in the right direction. Still not positive that isn't somewhat due to your decision to become a quasi-vegetarian, but we'll see. In any case, we're making progress. And once we find the real dog for the final cure, you'll be dead and it won't matter any longer. At least to you."

"I don't believe you," I said. "David Palmer must've realized you were completely insane, which is why he organized a coup. I'm on his side now."

"That's the losing side, Vic." Hal impatiently took his cellphone from me and scrolled back a bit, and showed off photos of me strapped to the lab table next to Jade, being humped by Brett. Then there were shots of me on a plane, presumably flying down to Houston, apparently loaded, laughing and goofing off, none of which gelled with my actual recollection of that murky time span. It all went back to my alcoholic blackouts, which I hadn't suffered in years. But I wasn't drinking *that* much. At least I didn't think so. There was something else going on. I believed Hal was spiking my brain as part of his "research."

And then there was Esmeralda Ava Margarita Valentina Valdez, a flesh-and-blood vision from beyond, suddenly showing up in a *lucha* mask a quarter century after our first encounter, somehow hooked into this whole devious scheme, even as a victim, but at that point, I couldn't be sure. Plus she was probably a vampire, at least of some sort. So was Jade. Even sitting there in the soft sunlight, she kept to the shady part of the patio. I could relate. I hated the sun, too. But I wouldn't suddenly burst into flames from overexposure to its oppressive rays. At least I haven't so far.

"None of this makes any sense," I said. "I don't see the point to any of it."

"Meaning what, Vic?" Hal said. "Life?"

"Well, that too. All this insanity fits into that inexplicable context, sure. I mean, not much makes sense anymore. But lately, I don't know. The world has gone completely mad. Zombies, cannibal dogs, bi-sexual vampire babes, fucking Donald Trump is the fucking president of the United States. It's all outside the realm of what I once considered reality. Now I don't know what to think." Then I looked at Val and said, "Or who to believe."

"Welcome to enlightenment," Hal said. "This corporeal world is an illusion. I mean, I have tons of pictures of Laura on my phone. Jade, too. They exist in my phone, but not in this world. Not any more. Just a little while ago, we could talk to them, touch them. They were real, tangible. Now they're not. So were they ever? Would you like to see them? Or at least their images?"

"See who, what?"

"The photos of Laura and Jade." Brett bristled slightly at her name, but didn't otherwise emote. "They're quite lovely," Hal said. "Taken in their prime, which was only a few days ago. Perfectly preserved for posterity."

I knew exactly what he meant, and my stomach churned. "No, thanks. How about Val? Any pictures of her?"

"*No,*" Val interjected emphatically. "Never. I am not one of his sex slaves. I'm only here to protect you from him, Vic. As long as I am here, you are safe."

"How's that?" I asked.

"Because he will not hurt me. Ever. He owes me for his life. And I want you alive."

"I see," I said, even though I was flying in the dark, as blind as a bat, virtually speaking. Just then I noticed one of my actual bats fly right through the patio, toward my room. I always left the window open to get whatever breeze there might be, since I didn't have one of the few air-conditioned rooms.

A moment later, Phantasia showed up and joined us. Hal didn't even react. But that didn't mean he wasn't as surprised as I was. He was just much better at hiding his feelings.

"How did you get here?" I asked her.

"I flew," she said matter-of-factly. Val kissed her, then poured her some coffee. I got a boner. At least it made me feel alive. Or at least awake.

"So toucans explode down here?" I asked Hal. "From the heat?"

"Only the ones I plant strategically, to create havoc," Hal said. "Another creation in our secret lab down here. It's a terrorism tactic. Random confusion breeds mass fear, which is how you control the masses. ISIL knows that. Every politician worth his fat paycheck knows that. I'm not a politician, just a businessman, but my business is making money, and to make money, you need to maintain dominance over the consumer public, tell them what to wear, what and whom to listen to, what to watch, how to live, how not to live, on and on. This way you can mass produce whatever garbage you want, and make them not only believe they want it, but need it. It's global capitalism at its purest and simplest. We profit off the chaos and confusion we breed and foster. It's been going on since the beginning of time, Vic. Or at least the dawn of civilization. I'm just taking it to the next level, expediting evolution, you might say."

"By spawning a zombie apocalypse?"

"No, ironically, that's what I'm trying to *prevent*. This present strain of the virus is an accidental mutation of our special blend of opioids and other secret ingredients, naturally cultivated then enhanced in the lab, carefully blended into various common household recipes, from dog food to dairy products to Daiquiris, ubiquitously distributed in order to infiltrate and infect the entire population, eventually. And by infect, I mean inject. The point of our products is to induce a kind of subconscious subservience to subliminal suggestion. We started with dogs since they're so susceptible to servitude, so we took advantage of their innate sense of loyalty, and literally fed them to each other, since it's more cost productive and sensible to recycle them than to just dump all the orphans in shelters, where they'll die anyway. Somehow the combination of dog meat with these chemicals and herbs, grown at my compound not far from here, induced a form of cannibalism in canines, which has proven infectious to humans. The question now is one of contagion. If that's the case, it defeats the purpose, which is to control and contain the general population."

So John Carpenter's *They Live* was prescient after all, just like *Network*. "Isn't creating mindless zombies the whole idea, you sick bastard?"

"Eventually, but I don't need literal zombies, Vic. That would be counterproductive, as I said. I need them alive and spending and worshipping and voting against their own interests. People at high levels in all fields and industries are nothing but clients and consumers to me. Or else they're my business partners. And everyone else are simply cattle to be exploited for profit. Not much different from the meat industry, really. We deny the lesser classes empathy the same way most of us deny the possibility of any sentient substance in the cows that get butchered and cooked into our hamburgers. Anyway, Vic, all of this process is just an inevitable if expedited evolution of an age-old paradigm that is about to reach its apex. But first, we have to work out the glitches. You, Vic, are nothing but a guinea pig, randomly selected, but then properly vetted for maximum benefit and minimized exposure, since you won't be missed when you're suddenly gone. Just like that poor sucker in Miami back in twenty-twelve. But you should feel grateful. Look at everything you've been able to experience in the past few days or weeks. More action and excitement than most people enjoy in a lifetime."

"You mean endure. I'm fucking miserable down here, totally out of my element. And I can't remember half of what you tell me I did. Even the stuff I can remember doesn't feel like it was really happened."

"That's why I began documenting everything, Vic. Well, one reason. The other, of course, is for our official research archives, preserved for the sake of future generations."

"Doesn't sound like they'll even care. How does Val fit into all of this?"

"Very well," Hal said with a wink. "I may owe her my life, but she owes me her career. So it evens out."

"Tell me," I said.

"I met Hal back in San Francisco, right after I met you," Val said.

"Ah-*hah*!" I blurted, Ralph Kramden-style. "You *do* remember me!"

"And I made good on my promise," she said quietly.

"It's all here!" Hal said, holding up his cellphone.

I grabbed for it, but Brett reflexively pushed me back down in my seat.

"I didn't want to involve you in this mess," Val said. "But now that I know you already are, there's no point in my charade. I honored our contract, even if you can't recall it, and saved your life. Just like I saved Hal's."

"How so?"

Hal jumped in: "I was crossing Powell Street and was almost run over by a cable car. Esmeralda, who was living there illegally at the time, I should mention, intervened and tackled me out of its path. I promised then and there to always take care of her, starting with her work visa. And so I have, ever since then. Like a sister."

"But not a *step*sister," I hoped out loud.

Hal smiled. "No, Vic. Esmeralda has never once acquiesced to my advances. I gave up long ago. Instead I set her up in business, first as a dancer in my club, and then via my many connections, a pro wrestler in Mexico City, where she is now famous, or should I say infamous, as 'La Loba.' I even introduced her to her little charge here. Didn't I, Phantasia?"

Phantasia nodded tersely without giving Hal eye contact. Hal just laughed.

"I don't understand why I've been complicit in all of this," I said. "It's like I've lost my will to live."

"That's part of it, but your midlife crisis, to put it in conventional terms, predates my entrance into your sad little pathetic nothing existence, Vic. But thanks to your unwitting participation, we're discovering that mixing alcohol with our brand of opioids induces blackouts and even comas, at least in some cases. You almost succumbed to that fate, but we were there to help you, since your usefulness had not yet come to an end."

"Like Dianne," I said.

"Dianne was setting me up per David," Hal said dismissively. By now he was repeating himself, like he was trying to convince his own conscience that all of his despicable actions were justified. I was sick of hearing it, but he kept chattering. Must've been how Val felt when I recited by life story. Karma was a bitch. "Dianne was just sleeping with me to make me think she was on my side," Hal continued, redundantly, "and I let her, but David and Dianne just wanted the business for themselves, then she wanted it all to herself, plus they considered some of my methods to be a little extreme. No vision, just ambition. They just wanted to make money. I have a much grander design in mind. Laura and Jade just wanted to save the dogs. Fucking bleeding heart animal lovers."

"I'm an animal lover, too. I hate humans. More now that ever.."

Hal laughed. "It's a natural hierarchy, Vic. Humans own this Earth. And the strong dominate the weak, in all species. Wasn't my idea. I didn't make the rules, but I do enforce them for the sake of the greater good."

"Meaning you and your chosen people."

"Tribalism is encoded in our DNA, Vic. There's no escaping it. Even wolves, which are essentially wild dogs, instinctively run in packs. But every tribe has a leader, because otherwise there would be no order. People don't just need to be contained as a group. Then *want* to be. Our new chemical ingredient, which can be mixed into any recipe without detection, is just a way to formalize and feed that natural desire."

"Consider me a lone wolf, then."

"Those are the ones that die first, you know."

"Sounds like an act of mercy, given the portrait you paint of society."

"That's a positive way of seeing it, yes. But not before the proper time. I'm running a business here."

"How far back does this set-up go?" I wondered aloud, asking anyone who might have an answer.

"I didn't plan any of this," Val said, and I believed her.

"That's always the best part of life," Hal said. "The surprises just around the corner. Keeps us interested and invested. Otherwise we'd just get bored, right? It's the unanswered questions that keep us going, along with our resistance to our own mortality."

"Why me?" I asked Hal, one last fucking time. "Of all the sorry saps in the world, why pick on me?"

"You're just fun to fuck with," Hal smiled.

That's when I finally lost it. I reached over and socked Hal in the mouth. When Brett stood up, I was about to kick him in the balls. Instead of blocking me, Brett followed up with a solid punch to Hal's head, knocking him out cold.

"Just go, and warn the world," Brett said, handing me Hal's phone, I assumed as evidence.

And so we did, with no destination in mind other than someplace else.

Chapter Thirteen
JUNGLE RUT

Phantasia drove us in her rented car out of the San Jose metropolitan area after informing us she was heading straight for the little town of Palmar Norte, exactly where I didn't want to go, since it was infested with zombies or whatever the hell they were. But it was her hometown, ironically enough, and she wanted to make sure her parents and siblings were safe, or saved, rather.

"I have the antidote," Phantasia told us. "The *real* one, made from the one and only dog's blood at David's lab in Houston."

Which meant I could be totally cured, too. But I wasn't immediately concerned about that. "So Fido is safe? Back in Texas?"

"No. He's someplace else. His blood was transported."

"But is he safe?"

"I don't know. All I know is he is somewhere in Costa Rica. That's where the blood came from, anyway."

"Shit." I was crestfallen. I didn't give a shit about the antidote, just the dog.

"We will find Fido," Val promised me. "That's part of the mission. We want to rescue *all* the test subjects, whether they walk on two or four legs. The main thing now is, Phantasia can begin curing the infected humans. You have enough?"

" A whole case of it," Phantasia said. "It's in the trunk. I was hiding it at our house in Mexico. Once you left, I followed you down as discreetly as possible."

"How will you administer it to all those people?" I

asked.

"Gas bombs. The virus can only be contracted via ingestion or shared bodily fluids, whether semen, saliva or blood, but the antidote can be mass produced and distributed as an airborne agent."

"Really? I didn't realize that was an optional method," I said. "Why didn't Hal just do that?"

"Because he's an asshole," Val said.

That simple answer explained so much about so many people in this world.

"Hal didn't seem surprised to see you," I observed.

"He doesn't reveal his true reactions to anything," Phantasia said. "That's how he stays one step ahead. Except this time, I got the drop on him. Brett was keeping me posted the whole time. He told me where to find you."

"So Brett gave you access to the antidote?" I asked.

"He's in love with me, or so he says. I might have to sleep with him later, but that's not important right now."

I looked at Val. "You have a problem with this?"

"With what?"

"Your girlfriend sleeping with Brett to save the planet. Or the town, anyway."

"No, why should I? And she's not my girlfriend. She's my sister."

"What?" Not *again*. "But you two made love back in Mexico. I saw you. Or heard you, anyway. So you mean *step*sister?"

Val rolled her eyes. "I'm speaking spiritually, Vic. The entire human race is bonded by biology, but separated by ideology. That's why the world is so fucked up. The point is, we're not blood relatives. Not in the conventional sense, anyway. We just live and sleep together. But neither has any hold over the other. We are free to do as we wish. If Phantasia can coax Brett to our side, I don't care how she accomplishes it. Men are idiots, anyway."

"So I've heard." I thought about what she told me.

Then I noticed the windows of the rented car were tinted. I just came right out and asked: "Are you vampires?"

They both laughed. "You have quite an imagination, Vic," Val said.

"Do I? I'm beginning to wonder where the lines are between illusion, delusion, and confusion."

"Believe whatever suits your preferred version of reality, Vic," Val said. "That's what everyone else does. That is why humanity needs religion. To answer the unanswerable, even if it's all only a theory. We see what we choose to see, and block out the rest."

"Like you pretending you didn't remember me," I said.

"I didn't want to deal with it right away, since I feel somewhat responsible for getting you into this mess. And then I was trying to figure out how to get you out of it."

"How so?"

"I'm the one that first told Hal about you."

I was crestfallen. Just like Raven, or even Rose, I thought: a powerful, dominating female with a big, broken heart that sent mixed signals via her conflicted conscience.

"So you're just another *femme fatale* in my life," I said with a sigh.

"Don't be sexist," Val said.

"How is that sexist?"

"You were on a list of potential subjects for Hal's research that I provided. I remembered you as being such a desperate, lonely little man back then, and for years after I first met you. Then I finally lost interest, and stopped tracking your whereabouts. But when I looked you up online again, I discovered you hadn't changed your lifestyle, just your address. Dianne was also keeping tabs on you, once you started walking that dog, which I didn't know at the time, but soon discovered through Laura and Jade, who were working with me. We're in the same organization."

"The secret one Jade told me about."

"Yes. I recruited them, indirectly, by planting them inside Hal's empire, in different roles, once I discovered Hal was feeding dog meat to dogs, and human meat to humans, essentially commercializing cannibalism. But by then I was in too deep, per our arrangement. When I confronted him directly, he threatened to kill Phantasia if I interceded or narced on him. I told him I'd only go along if you were kept safe, while my sisters continued to work their own internal angles. Hal only promised to delay your death and make it as painless as possible. That's the best deal I could get."

"Well, if I die, at least I got to reconnect with you," I said to Val.

She actually teared up. "The most circuitous routes are often more rewarding than the direct paths," she said. "Because once you arrive at your destination, you feel like you've really earned it."

"Did we really make love?" I asked.

"Yes."

"I didn't see those pictures on Hal's phone."

"I deleted them when he was asleep in our room. I was just hoping he wouldn't notice. If he did, too late now. At least for him."

"Why did you delete them? At least I'd have a memento. And *proof*."

"Because I didn't want them in Hal's possession. He wants to own me, own everyone and everything. It gives him the illusion of control, even though he understands and accepts it's all a mirage anyway. But he settles for the temporary feeling of power. Anyway, that moment could not belong to him. It was too special for me to allow that."

"It was?"

"You really don't remember? Or are you just trying to get back at me, for pretending to forget our deal."

"No, I mean it. I can't remember any of it. Maybe it wouldn't have lived up to the hype after so long, anyway."

She leaned over close and said softly, "Maybe we'll

have to recreate it sometime, then." And then she kissed me. My boner nearly burst through my already severely soiled new slacks, which were no longer white, but sort of an impressionistic painting due to the various stains it incurred since leaving Mexico.

"So you gave up being a detective after you didn't find your long lost love?" Phantasia asked, purposely stepping on the moment, perhaps out of jealousy, but mostly to mess with me. I just brought that out in people, I guess.

"No, not until a couple of years ago, after moving to Seattle," I said. "Though truthfully, it was a long, slow fade. I wasn't doing it that much anymore, even in San Francisco. I mostly made a living as a bouncer and freelance burlesque booking agent. Now I'm a dog walker."

"Do you like it?"

"It suits me. I dig the company."

"I understand."

"Everyone is a detective," Val said. "We're all seeking the truth. The ultimate truth, which renders all other mundane mysteries moot."

She was so wise. And hot. "I'm totally in love with you," I said.

"I know," she replied.

That was a pretty big bowl of *albondigas* left hanging out there.

Once we were back in Palmar Norte, it was like I'd never left. Lingering clouds of smoke, stray dogs and aimlessly wandering zombies were still permeating the place. We walked through and tossed the gas bombs left and right, making the air that much denser. The antidote was harmless to the non-infected, but almost instantly cured the infected, including whatever remnants of the virus remained in our own systems. To tell the truth, I didn't feel any different after I inhaled the stuff. But then I lived my entire life in a hazy daze.

In about an hour, the streets were littered with confused citizens, jabbering in Spanish. They had no memory of what had happened to them, which was another merciful benefit of the antidote. I thought of all the victimized patrons back at Casa de la Gata, being brutally beaten to death by Roy and Brett.

"Why didn't Brett just gas bomb the nightclub and save everyone?" I asked.

"He didn't actually kill anyone," Phantasia explained. "Brett and Roy were just knocking them out, though with some head injuries for sure, to make it seem like they were killing them. Brett is there now, distributing the antidote. Hal actually locked them all inside, to deal with later. But they'll just wake up and remember only a vague nightmare. Hal won't have the opportunity to check on them, anyway."

"Where is Hal now?"

"Brett took him to David," Phantasia informed me.

"So everyone is turning on Hal," I said. "All at once."

"Yes," said Val. "Power in numbers. He's gone completely insane, and he must be stopped and punished. That's our single common goal. Once that is achieved, then we take down David."

"But why did so many people go along with him to begin with?"

"He's been giving us little doses of hypnotic hallucinogen," Val explained. "Even you. Your drinks, your food, your sex."

"What?"

"Jade began infecting you back in Vancouver. When you ate her pussy, you consumed some of the virus in fluid form. It was in her juices."

I suppressed my boner. "But I thought Hal injected me in the scrotum with the antidote?"

"That's wasn't an antidote. Just the next phase of the virus." (I called it!) "He was experimenting with dosage. For some reason even a little of the drug mixed into dog food takes total effect when ingested by canines, and then they pass it on full strength to humans. But when it goes from human to human, it's being filtered by the human immune system somehow, stripping it of its potency. So the test subjects, including you, would require multiple doses to maximize the ultimate impact, given the inexplicable dilution. But unfortunately, his people have created a much more concentrated formula, which is what he planted in the nightclub food and drinks. Also here, in this town. So apparently it now works when dispensed in large batches. Now they're no doubt working on a slightly less potent formula, that will only induce subliminal hypnosis, not cannibalistic characteristics, though actually, the subjects so far have only partially eaten their own victims, which means it's already regressing to the original form of mutation."

"Like the one in Miami back in twenty-twelve."

"Exactly, that one escaped the lab. The more recent subjects, meaning the ones that weren't even aware they were in an experiment, unlike you, just wanted to infect the uninfected, due to their innate tribalistic instincts. Hal is counting on our common fallacies as a species to expedite the process of mass slavery via subliminal hypnosis, which marketers, politicians and religious leaders have been implementing for centuries, though not quite so diabolically and directly."

"So, to sum all this up, when Hal's folks come up with the perfectly balanced formula, he will turn the world's population into zombies, at least just enough to control them."

"This is why we have to stop all this madness, here and now, before he's able to start spiking the entire world's food population. Then there won't be enough of the antidote available to quell this silent plague, stop it from spreading without anyone suspecting, since the antidote, created by the same scientists, can't yet be produced on such a scale, then distributed with equal effectiveness."

"You sound like you know what you're talking about."

"I have a medical degree, Vic. Also a PhD in Psychology. Which comes in handy with you, I must say."

"Really? Where did you graduate?"

"Berkeley, on a student visa which expired, so Hal arranged a work visa for me. But I grew up mostly in Japan. That's why I don't have an accent."

"Was your father in the military or something?"

"Or something."

"Why didn't you become a psychologist or doctor instead of a masked wrestler and exotic dancer?"

"It's too cerebral. I'm not one for academics, I discovered. I'm too physical. I crave action. But my education helps me in other, more practical ways."

"I'm a high school dropout and a middle-aged dog walker."

"Yes, I know. I know all about you, Vic. I've been keeping tabs on you all this time, remember."

"You're even a better detective than I am."

"That's a low bar, but yes."

"Why didn't you just call me?"

"I did. Many times."

The Phone Phantom. "So that *was* you leaving those messages on my machine? The old songs?"

"Yes," she confessed.

"Why didn't you just come out from the shadows and contact me?"

"Wrong time, wrong president."

"But what were the odds Donald Trump would ever actually be president?"

"Pretty long, that's why I pulled that out of my ass."

"And a fine ass it is. Lousy deal, though."

"Really? I made good on it. I'm always true to my word, Vic. One reason I kept you on my radar, just in case. Now, as Damon Runyon would say, my marker is paid in full."

175

"So you say. You destroyed the evidence."

"We'll make new evidence when this is all over."

"Promise?"

She shook on it. I knew she was a woman of honor now. Well, I hoped, anyway.

"One last thing," I said.

"Yes."

"Ivar."

"Who?"

"The sailor statue. The one that's been haunting me since I got to Seattle. That was you, right?"

"I don't know anything about that, Vic."

"But I saw him, Val."

"Don't call me that. My name is Esmeralda."

"I like calling you Val. Just like I named the sailor statue Ivar, after the restaurant chain in Seattle. What did you call him?"

"I didn't call him anything. I told you, I don't even know what you mean."

"Val, Esmeralda, whatever, I saw him, or it, back at your place in Mexico City. The sailor statue. *You* know. C'mon. You already copped to the phantom phone messages. Why hold back on this?"

"I'm not holding back on anything, Vic. I have no such statue in my home. Now, let's go. We have a stop to make and then we're on to Hal's compound."

"To do what?"

"Take it down," Phantasia said. She was carrying three automatic weapons of some sort, which she'd just taken from a gun shop on the corner. Or a shop that sold guns, anyway. I got the idea she didn't actually purchase them, though. Beautiful women get a lot of free shit, especially from stupid men, like me.

"What do you mean, take it down?"

Phantasia handed me a gun, then said, "You know what I mean. Time to end all of this, Vic. First we have to go back and pick up Brett from the club. He will join us in the final battle."

I balked. "I don't like the sound of that. Either 'final' or 'battle,' but especially in the same sentence."

Val whispered in my ear, "But I'll be waiting at the end of this bloody road, Vic. Naked and ready."

"Load 'n' lock," I said, taking the gun from Phantasia.

They just looked at me and laughed, though as usual, I wasn't sure why. So I laughed along with them, which just made them laugh more.

Brett was at a little stand around the corner from the motel, eating *ceviche,* when we rolled up in the rental car.

"Try this," Brett said to me. "I'll buy you one. Best in the world."

Brett asked the ladies behind the counter for three more orders. He was right. We all sat eating the best damn *ceviche* in the world, washed down with damn good *cerveza.*

Then we started back to the motel to switch vehicles, because, I assumed, taking a rental car on a raid might not be covered in the insurance policy. I asked Brett where he was from. He told me New Orleans. He didn't seem much for small talk. So I enlarged the topic of conversation.

"Why are you doing this?" He just nodded ahead at Phantasia.

"That's it? That's all it took?"

"Love is all that matters, Vic. I know that now."

I nodded. "Oh. Well, good for you."

"That's the secret, Vic. To everything."

"If only it was that easy."

"It is, Vic. Just hard to see sometimes."

"I see."

"No, you don't."

"I meant…yeah. You're right."

I just hoped Phantasia returned Brett's affections. As if reading my mind, he said, "I'm going to marry her so I can become a citizen of Costa Rica. I mean legally. I want to stay here and run my writers retreat. This will be my new home base."

"Does she know that?"

"Not yet, but she will. She wants to stay here, too."

"But she's become a resident of Mexico, I thought."

"No, she's actually from here. Are you saying you can't tell the difference between a Mexican and a Costa Rican?"

"Oh, no. No, no. Of course not. I mean, yeah."

"You know what else?"

I was afraid. "No, what."

Brett nodded at Val, just ahead of us, holding hands with Phantasia. I bet they could hear us, but were pretending not to.

"Esmeralda wants to go back to the states, badly, but she can't."

"Trump's immigration policies?"

"Partly. She needs a sponsor."

"You mean a green card. By marriage. To a U.S. citizen."

Brett just smiled, for the first time in my presence. It creeped me out. But I let the seed he planted in my head start growing, then and there.

"Hal proposed to her many times, but she always turned him down. She doesn't want to marry just anyone. She's picky. So maybe you'll be the lucky one, if you play your cards right."

"Where's Hal now, anyway?" I asked him. Now that I knew he had wanted to marry her, I needed confirmation that competition had been completely eliminated.

"Somewhere he can't hurt anyone, at least for now."

"I want a piece of him."

"Don't worry, I'll save you a slice."

I wasn't sure exactly what that meant, but it didn't sound too appetizing.

Once I was back in my room, there was a knock at the door. I looked up and didn't see the bats.

Val walked in, and shut the door behind her. "Don't tell Brett, but Phantasia is not bi-sexual. She's a full-on lesbian."

Suddenly I felt like I was on a Mexican soap opera. "Okay…"

"I'm only telling you because things may look weird in a little bit."

"You mean weird*er*."

"But there's a plan. There's always a plan, and things are never what they seem."

"Tell me about it."

"I am."

"Brett is only doing this to win her over, you know," I said. "He just told me."

"No, he's not. It's really for his brother. It has been all along"

"His brother?"

"Yes. Gary Thornton Palmer."

"You mean the late Gary in Vancouver is, or was, Brett's brother?"

"Yes."

Another god damn wrinkle in this already twisted tapestry. "Which means David Palmer is Brett's stepfather, and that makes Dianne his… *mother*?"

"Yes. That is another reason. It's not just a vendetta. It's a family business thing, You see, Brett, Laura, and Jade were secretly working with David, trying to keep Hal from finding the dog, so they could develop and secure the antidote themselves. At the same time, Jade, Laura and I were plotting against David as well. When Hal had Gary killed, Dianne decided to turn on him, too, even though she was sleeping with him, though when David found out about the affair, Dianne told him she was working undercover."

"Under the covers, anyway."

"Well, he bought it, anyway. Then Dianne kept tabs on Hal for David, who was working at cross-purposes with our organization, since we just wanted to save the dogs from being turned into food for their own kind. I tried telling David that Dianne ultimately wanted to take over the entire organization herself, which meant killing him, too, but he didn't believe me."

"I still don't understand how any of you really thought Hal could be fooled with this conspiracy. I mean, I can't even follow it, and I'm writing it all down, at least mentally. But then my head hurts and I get confused easily."

"Hal has no idea David is Brett's stepfather, or that Dianne was his real mother."

"So Brett must hate Hal for not only killing his brother and mother, but plotting against his stepdad. That's a lot of built-up resentment."

"Yes. And Jade was his true love, so that just quadruples his lust for vengeance. Until he met Phantasia. She has softened his heart."

"You mean hardened his dick."

"Whatever works."

"But she is only going to break his heart again."

"Not before she sleeps with him. She feels like she owes him that much. She knows how to make a man happy. You should know."

"Wait. You know she slept with me?"

"Yes. I know everything, Vic. I am always watching, remember that. But she was still pretending to do Hal's bidding then. Or else, no fucking way. You're not her type. I am."

"Well, I wasn't in love her. Brett *is*. Sleeping with him just to square a debt will only make it worse."

"It will be good for his writing."

"You mean like Ava Gardner breaking Sinatra's heart is what made him *Sinatra*."

"If that helps you."

"Hey, I'm not the one that needs help. Anyway, what happens after this is all over, provided we survive?"

She kissed me quickly and said, "I don't want to spoil the surprise."

And I don't want it to spoil me, I thought.

We drove in Brett's black, intimidating, militaristic Hummer deep into the jungle somewhere, don't ask me where, I had no clue. All I know is it was about an hour's drive from San Jose, but it seemed like we were deep, deep in the middle of the densest hellhole on Earth.

On the way, I happened to mention to Brett that I was sad to hear about Gary and Dianne. "He seemed like a nice guy, and she was a real sweetheart," I lied. Everyone's better qualities were magically magnified post-mortem, anyway. Naturally, I neglected to mention that I was literally a motherfucker.

Brett shot Val, who was sitting next to me in the back seat, a certain look via the rear view mirror, and she ricocheted it right at me, elbowing me in the rib. "That's none of your business," he said tersely.

"So that means Laura was your stepsister, yes?"

"Yes, another reason I hated Hal. Having her killed, then blaming her death, as well as Jade's, on me, at least to you, but probably just to mess with my head, or smoke me out, if he somehow suspected my roots. Though honestly, Laura and I were never that close, at least as family."

I wanted to ask if he'd ever tag-teamed on Laura with Gary, but frankly, I figured I was better off not knowing for sure.

"Why did the cowboys try to kill Hal back in Houston if they were working for him?"

"They weren't. They were trying to kill me and my mother. They got her but missed me. Hal overplayed his hand. But I didn't let him know I knew. You were considered more or less expendable at that point, since you were marked for death anyway, and Hal figured the antidote would work, so you'd outlived your usefulness."

"Yeah, since birth. How did you hide all this from Hal?"

"'Brett Wheeler' is just one of my many aliases. My mother introduced us, but didn't reveal our connection. I was basically working undercover for my stepdad, who never trusted Hal. I was keeping tabs and filing reports behind his back. Hal had no idea who my father was, and it's hard keeping a secret from that guy. Or it was. Anyway, I wasn't too happy when Hal ordered my brother hit, but I didn't find out till it was too late."

"Wait a minute. You and Jade were working together against Hal, for your stepdad?" I asked, pretending Val hadn't already informed me of this. I just needed confirmation since I still wasn't sure who was lying to me, and who wasn't. Even Val was suspect at that point, though I was willing to forgive her. Plus I didn't want Brett to start wondering about Val's true allegiance, which wasn't to David Palmer.

"Yeah," Brett said. "I was in Vancouver to bring you back to Minneapolis. But that's when Jade suddenly split up with me, probably because she knew Hal was going to kill Gary, though we'd been having our problems before that. I went back to Minneapolis by myself. I didn't find out Gary was dead till just before you both arrived there, so naturally things were tense, especially since I couldn't show my hand in front of Hal yet. And Jade was complicit by not protecting him. I have to admit, that helped me get over her. I think that's why she let it happen, frankly. But also to protect her cover. Wasn't worth my brother's life, though. Not to me. I almost threw in the towel when Gary died. But now I have something to live for." He then looked at Phantasia in the passenger seat, who just smiled back at him. Val was glaring at me to keep my mouth shut, and so I did for the duration of the trip.

We finally reached a fenced-off, secluded area, and through the thicket of trees I saw the secret lab. It wasn't that impressive, at least not on the outside. It looked more like an old factory converted to a makeshift headquarters for a rogue community on *The Walking Dead* than, say, a sleek super-villain hideout from a Bond movie. But then "Hal" wasn't exactly a Bond villain kind of name, though he was very calm and calculated, like a certain computer.

I looked up and noticed the place was surrounded by toucans that didn't move.

"Are those toucans actually bird-bombs?" I asked anyone.

"No, they're macaws," Val said. "But yes, they're bombs."

I didn't know the difference between a macaw and a toucan, but I did know the difference between a macaw and a bomb. Except when the bomb looked like a macaw. Or a toucan or whatever the fuck.

"Definitely, set to go off if we trigger some kind of warning sensor, probably," Brett said.

By then, an uploaded amateur tourist video of the exploding toucans back at Playa Ventanas had gone viral. Val showed me on the ride over. Most people assumed it was a practical joke, since no one was actually hurt. Brett assured us these particular deadly robot birds were rigged with more powerful explosives, since their purpose was to maim and kill, not confuse and disrupt.

"So how do we know when we set one off?" I asked.

"It will blow up," Brett whispered. "They're like land mines, except they're in the trees, and we don't need to actually touch one to detonate it."

"How do you know?"

"I helped Hal design and plant them. I was in the Marines. Special Ops. Iraq, Afghanistan. This is why he hired me. Plus I know forty-two different ways to kill someone with my bare hands."

I nodded, grateful he was on our side, even if it was temporary. I just wanted him to be my pal until I got safely on a plane back to Seattle.

Then I noticed Val and Phantasia had donned their *lucha* masks. Phantasia's mask was multi-colored, in contrast to Val's trademark solid gold mask. Otherwise they both wore halter tops, tight shorts, and hiking boots. They looked like superheroes. Brett was wearing standard combat gear, including a flak jacket, probably left over from his soldier days. I was wearing a badly stained *guayabera* and torn slacks. My *huaraches* were all messed up, too. With the semi-automatic rifle strapped to my shoulder, I felt a little more prepared, but not much. Especially since I was unprotected from any return fire. That didn't seem to be of any concern to anyone other than myself.

"Don't kill anyone," Brett said. "They won't be armed and there are no guards on duty right now. There are security camera, and an alarm, but that's fine, I can take those out quickly. Once we're in, just shoot around the people. They won't put up a fight, trust me. Just a bunch of nerds. The idea is to startle them into total submission, so we can then target the proper facilities."

"With what?" I asked.

"These," Brett said, opening up a sack of hand grenades. "You know how to use these, right, Vic?"

"Um…I've seen it done in a few movies. You just pull that thing there and chuck it, right?"

"Right, but only when you're ready to throw it. Otherwise you'll blow yourself up and maybe us as well. Once we're inside, I'll tell you where to toss 'em. If we all spread out, we can take out all the processors in under a minute. I've been inside so I know where they all are. Ready?"

"Um…"

"Let's go!"

With that, Brett opened the fence, since he knew the

combination to the lock, and we stormed inside the building.

Val yelled, "Nobody move!" Then all three of them fired their weapons into the air as warning shots. I was going to but I was late on the draw and didn't want to be redundant. A bunch of geeks wearing lab coats raised their hands and backed off in a huddle, looking at Brett with expressions ranging from disbelief to anger. "Drums-a-Go-Go" was pounding in my head. I felt like I was in Ted V. Mikels' *The Doll Squad*, except there were two men on the assault team. Well, one and a half, anyway.

Just then a mob of zombies came lunging at us from a back room, like the ones in 1955's *Creature with the Atom Brain*. Probably subjects kept around for further experimentation as well as protection in a situation like this. One of the lab geeks had opened a door to let them out, I guess. There were maybe a dozen of them, all obviously involuntarily incarcerated and infected. Phantasia lobbed some antidote gas bombs at them, and they collapsed, then got back up, completely disoriented, but otherwise back to normal, which I supposed was an improvement from their perspective.

Then we noticed a cage full of scared, barking dogs. We opened it up and they took off in every direction, happily emancipated, probably to be adopted by local residents. They all looked like Fido. He would probably be among them, as one of the ongoing test subjects. How would I know him if I actually found him?

The same way I "found" Rose: Fido found *me*.

He ran up to me and I scooped him up and held him close with one arm, my machine gun in the other. I felt like a proud papa when he licked my face in gratitude.

As I held Fido, I noticed a statue sitting up on a shelf. It was my old pal Ivar, looking down on the scene with omniscient bemusement. I chalked it up to one of my many hallucinations caused by the drugs in my system, though it looked real to me. Reality had become relative, though.

Once the room was clear, Brett handed out grenades like they were party favors, and told us what to target. I held Fido even tighter as I lobbed the grenades, to shield him from the explosions. He still shivered and whined, though, and I felt lousy about it.

I also felt great, since there I was: blowing shit up in Latin America. I guess I was kind of like James Bond after all. We both probably had fucked up livers, anyway. But in truth, I was more like Jonny Quest.

After we'd blown all the shit up, we ran outside, behind the fleeing test subjects and scientists and dogs, just as the entire place exploded behind us in a chemical chain reaction, or so I assumed. The whole scene was so hectic there wasn't much time for analysis. I felt like we were running in slow motion. Just like in every stupid action movie ever made. It was glorious. I felt exhilarated. Terrified, but exhilarated.

At least until we ran smack into a brigade of scary-looking armed badasses, wearing shades and dark clothes, one of whom ordered us to drop our weapons. Only we didn't. Okay, I did, but then I picked it right back up when I saw nobody else had. I just wasn't sure what the right thing to do was in these situations. I mean, in reality, which wasn't my preferred realm. Apparently the world inside my head and the one outside had merged without my consent.

"David's private police force," Brett informed us. "But I guess they betrayed him. Everyone has a fucking price. Bastards. He was good to you." Then Brett paused ominously before asking, almost rhetorically, "Where's David?"

Then from behind some of the men, out stepped Hal, laughing. "Right here, sonny boy." There was an audible gasp, probably from me. Hal snapped his fingers and one of the goons stepped out carrying a bloody human head on a stick, Alfredo Garcia-style, then planted it in the ground like a gory tiki torch, engulfed by swarming flies.

"Holy fuck," I whispered, clinging to Fido.

Val screamed, Phantasia vomited. Brett was visibly upset, at last, but was holding back till an opportunity to properly react presented itself. Or he created one.

Then things happened quickly. Hal, smiling as usual, clicked some kind of device in his hand and the macaws in the trees all started exploding at once. The actual toucans took off. Or maybe they were also macaws. I'd lost track by then. I was too focused on protecting poor little Fido from any further trauma.

Everyone dashed for cover behind the trees and started shooting at each other, as bullets, shattered shards of bark, and dust filled the air between the adversaries. Except for me. I just hid in some bushes, to shield Fido, or so I told myself. I really wasn't a gun guy, especially a machine gun guy. I had carried a .38 for years and it often came in handy. Right now I was just looking up at the trees, trying to discern the difference between macaws and toucans. Basically, macaws are red parrots. Toucans have long yellow bills. While I was figuring this out, everyone else kept shooting at each other. If only they'd just stop and look at the birds, everything would be fine.

At one point, Phantasia reached behind her waist, pulled out a knife, and threw it hard at Hal, hitting him right in the throat. The sudden act momentarily stunned and confused the dirty cops, which was no doubt part of the extemporaneous plan. As blood bubbled from Hal's neck and he fell, Brett wiped out the rest of the distracted regimen with a few well-targeted rounds. Val rested against a tree as Phantasia consoled her. I got the idea Val wasn't a natural born killer like the others.

Brett went over to Hal and lifted his head up, resting it on his knee. I walked over and spit on Hal as he bled to death.

"Ow," Hal said sarcastically. No one ever took me seriously.

"You killed my stepfather," Brett said bitterly. "And my brother. And mother. *And* sister."

"*Step*sister," Hal corrected him.

Brett sat back, stunned. "You mean you fucking *knew*? The whole fucking time?"

Hal laughed, spitting up blood. "You gotta be kidding, punk," he said in a raspy voice. "I know everything. You were supposed to die in that bar, too. But I had Jade killed, which I knew would be the same as killing you, too."

That was when Brett, his face flush and his eyes filled with tears, began strangling Hal, causing more blood to pump from the gash in his neck.

Phantasia pulled Brett off and said, "Stop it! You're blocking my view! I want to *watch* that motherfucker *die*!"

"I love you," Hal said to Brett in a gurgling whisper. "All of you. It's all about love. I know that now."

"Shut up and die already," Val said.

Hal did as he was told. Finally.

With Fido tucked safely beneath one arm, I went over and planted a big kiss on Val's luscious lips. "You're my hero," I told her.

"And you're mine," she smiled. I didn't know why, but I took it.

Brett was carrying Hal's body as we headed back to the Hummer. We just left the dead goons on the ground to be eaten by the local carnivorous wildlife, thereby contributing to the ecosystem, so their lives weren't a total waste. The subjects were freed to get back home on their own. The dogs were also set loose to run wild or more likely get adopted by natives, or even some of the scientists, who may have formed an attachment for them despite the experimentation. Brett just dumped Hal's body in the back of the Hummer like it was a sack of shit. Which I guess it was. However, I have to admit, I agreed with Hal on a number of philosophical points. I shared his misanthropy, for one thing, though I stopped short of acting on it. And real life zombies were something I never thought I'd witness, so I owed him that, too. George Romero never lived to see it, either. It was all so sad, really. And yet so fucking cool in a sick way. My emotions were conflicted, to say the least. I would need time to process all this, at home in Seattle, with Fido and Doc and a Martini at my side.

Back at Melrost Airport Bed and Breakfast, we all collected our luggage, or rather, everyone else did. All I was bringing back was Fido, which was the only baggage that mattered to me. Brett said everyone needed to get out of town fast, because the cops loyal to Hal would be looking for us, even though Val and Phantasia had been wearing masks, leaving Brett and me the fall guys. He didn't seem that worried about it, though. The scientists were there under duress, he explained, so we'd emancipated them, making it less likely they'd cooperate with authorities.

Val didn't seem too happy about being a cop killer, or a dirty cop killer, or any kind of killer, period, even if it was in self-defense, though something told me this wasn't her first time. I figured I'd ask her about it later. Brett and Phantasia didn't seem fazed by their homicidal rampage, both apparently hardened by past experience with similar situations. They had that much in common, at least. Still, Brett's penis was probably a deal breaker, romance-wise. I just didn't have the heart to tell him.

Once we'd quickly packed, Brett was ready to drive Val and me to the airport. Phantasia stayed behind. Together, employing some of David Palmer's loyal employees (as far as Brett knew), they were going to transform the land that the secret lab once occupied, which was Palmer property on paper, into a writer's colony, rebuilt from scratch. The name of the area was San Buenas, I found out later.

I was amazed how easy it seemed for Val to part with her lover (and mine, that once). They simply embraced and cried a bit as they said their goodbyes, but that was it.

"I can't believe you're not more emotional," I said to Val. "I mean, about leaving Phantasia. Unless that's why you were crying."

"No, that wasn't it. And this isn't goodbye forever, simply *hasta la vista*."

"No? You'll be…coming back?"

"Oh no, I'm finished here, but she'll come visit me in the States, once the colony is up and running."

"The States. For good?"

"Of course. That's always been my dream."

"What part? I hear Seattle is nice this time of year, now that autumn is around the corner. I'm so sick of this damn heat. Can't wait to get back."

"I'm going to Hawaii."

My spirits sank. "Why Hawaii? I thought you hated the sun, just like me?"

"I do. I don't want to settle there. I just want to go for my honeymoon. Just like in my favorite movie, 'Blue Hawaii.'"

She was an Elvis fan on top of everything else. But that fact took a backseat to the other bombshell she'd just dropped on me from out of the blue. "You're getting married?"

"Yes."

"To who?"

"To any sap that can make me a legal U.S citizen."

Since I was doubtlessly the biggest sap she'd ever met, I took the bait. "Can I volunteer for duty?"

She kissed me passionately and grabbed my crotch. I took that as a yes. But my boner was gone. I figured it just needed a rest after all this excitement. I'd save it for the honeymoon.

After all, I was officially engaged for the first time in my life. Something else I never thought would happen, on top of zombies. In fact, my bride to be was a vampire. Maybe. I was downright giddy. But this wasn't the only reason I was beside myself.

"I can't believe I just helped save the world," I said as we loaded up.

"Not really," said Brett. "You just happened to be there when we did."

"I'm the one that hit Hal back at the motel and got this ball rolling."

"I was about to hit him," Brett said. "Or Esmeralda was. You just beat us to it."

"Aw, c'mon, can't I get some credit at least?"

Val smiled as she stroked my hair and said, "Comic relief."

"Well, that's something, at least," I said.

"Yes," she said. "It's something all right." Then she kissed me and that made it all worthwhile. At least I got the girl in the end, for once.

When we left for the airport, there was still a corpse hidden in the back of the Hummer, beneath some blankets, adding to the overall surreality of everything.

"So what are you going to do with Hal's body?" I asked Brett.

"The body? Dump it. They only want the head."

"Who does?"

Brett just looked at me and said, "You don't want to know."

He was right. I didn't. That might spoil the moment.

Chapter Fourteen
PARADISE, WHININ' STYLE

We didn't fly straight to Honolulu. We bought tickets for Houston, so I could pick up Doc. Val bought a carrier for Fido in San Jose. Now Fido and Doc would be pals. And stepbrothers, once we made it legal. Hopefully that didn't mean they'd start humping each other, but whatever. I didn't even care if Val didn't actually love me and was using me to become a U.S. citizen. Just the novelty of actually exchanging wedding vows, especially at this relatively late stage of the game, was too much for me to resist. And at least we'd have some kind of bond, for a while, anyway. I didn't even want to consider a life without her now. But as usual, I'd take whatever I could get.

On the plane ride over, Val psychoanalyzed me. It was part of the domestic service, I guess. I scored quite a package deal, mentally, spiritually, and of course physically speaking, though I hadn't experienced a boner since leaving Costa Rica, which was worrying me. Maybe we needed to vacation in Viagra Falls. But just looking at Val was probably all the therapy I needed. Sexually, anyway. She was taking care of the rest of me, too.

I told her how I was such a romantic putz when I was younger, then I morphed into a gigolo as I aged. I chalked it up to my apathetic attitude, which I achieved the hardest way possible. It certainly wasn't my physique or male prowess. She concurred, but added:

"Woman love you because we can tell you worship and respect us. Even though you do objectify our bodies. Underlying that is a sincere sweetness, as well as a little lost puppy quality that appeals to our maternal instincts, no matter the age gap. Plus you're gullible and easy to manipulate."

"Hm," I said. That didn't exactly instill me with confidence, considering she was going to be my wife, at least legally. I was in no position to be picky. I didn't even ask her if she loved me, since she still hadn't done more than acknowledge my proclamation of devotion back at the motel. She was growing quieter and more pensive, too. What was I getting myself into, and more importantly, how could I keep from getting out of it?

After obtaining our Harris County marriage certificates, Val and I were wed at Houston Municipal Court House, surrounded by my adopted Texas family, as well as Doc and Fido. We even hired a local mariachi band, just to play "Mia Manera (My Way)" after the brief ceremony.

There were tears and hugs and then we returned to the scene of the crime, literally: Lei Low, which had reopened since the Texas Tiki Bar Massacre. We all wanted to pave over that one very bad memory with more good ones.

Val and I danced to "Can't Help Falling in Love" by Elvis, which we designated as "our song." Then we drank and cussed and drank some more. They were the bawdiest, naughtiest Christian conservatives I'd ever met. I was proud to call them my extended adoptive family. But I was also anxious to get back to my real home, with my real family.

We went back to Mina's house in Pearland or maybe it was Carol's house in Friendswood, I don't know, and ate and drank some more. Val and I passed out on a guest bed with Fido and Doc cuddling at our feet.

Then the next morning we finally flew back to Seattle. Home, sweet home. Even if it was only a pitstop on the way to Paradise, Hawaiian Style.

When we arrived at my apartment, three members of the biker gang, The Emerald City Wizards, were standing there waiting for us. I wondered if they'd been there the whole time I was away.

In any case, they were there for Fido. I clutched onto his carrier as Val held Doc in his. There was a lot of barking and meowing. I felt like joining the chorus.

"Mickey wants his dog back," one said emphatically.

"It's not even his dog," I said. "It belongs to some Russian."

"Right. And now the Russian wants his dog back, but from Mickey."

"Well, I'm not giving him up, so there."

One punched me in the face, but Val quickly disabled him with a karate chop to the throat with her free hand. Then she kicked another in the shins while getting the third in a headlock and kneeing him in the face after setting down the cat carrier. Doc was screeching. But then one biker drew a knife, another a gun, and that was that. They took Fido out of his crate by force. Then one grimaced and said, "This isn't Mickey's dog!"

"Yes, it is!" I insisted.

"No it's *not*!"

"Get the fuck outta here!"

"Y*ou* get the fuck outta here! This is so not the right fucking dog, you idiot!"

"Is so!"

"Is not!"

"Is *so*!" I took Fido from the biker's muscular arms and examined him. He looked and acted just like Fido. The original, one and only Fido. He even licked my face affectionately for confirmation.

"See? He loves me!" I said.

One of the bikers took Fido's left paw in his big, hairy hand, and said, "There's no white spot. Mickey's dog had a white spot on his left paw."

I tried rubbing the paw in case it was dirty or something, but no. This wasn't Fido after all. I began to get emotional. What happened to the *real* Fido?

Val just looked at me, shaking her head. All that, and Fido was still lost.

One of the bikers shoved his fat finger in my face. "Where is Mickey's dog?"

"I don't know," I said truthfully. "I think maybe he's down in Costa Rica somewhere."

"Costa fucking *Rica*?" another biker exclaimed. "What the fuck is he doing down there!?"

"Go fucking get him!" demanded another one, grabbing me by the throat.

Val karate chopped his arm and he let go. He tried to hit her but she punched him first, then kicked his nuts, and he went down. My private shrink was also my bodyguard. I had hit the proverbial jackpot.

But then the other two pointed their weapons at us threateningly. We were unarmed. It was a Seattle standoff.

"Look, this is the wrong dog," Val said diplomatically. "We're sorry, but the other one is gone."

I teared up just thinking about it.

"He probably found a good home with one of the scientists," Val assured me.

"What fucking scientists?" a biker said.

Just then my ancient landlady came out and looked at us sternly. "Will you all please keep it down? I'm trying to watch my show." She was seemingly, perhaps willfully, oblivious to the gun, the knife, and the seriousness of the situation.

We all just stared back at her. "Thanks for watching Doc while I was gone," I said sardonically.

"You're welcome," she said, closing the door. She didn't even realize he'd been missing. Not a very reliable pet sitter. I guessed from now on I'd have to take Doc with me wherever I went. And Fido, too. Even if this wasn't the original Fido. I wondered what we'd do with them while on our honeymoon. If we lived that long, anyway.

But it turned out okay. Once my landlady (I keep

forgetting her name, sorry) shut the door, the bikers just gave up.

"What are you going to tell Mickey?" I asked.

"That you lost his dog," one said with a shrug.

"Does that mean you'll be back?" I said.

"Better leave town for a while," another one admonished as they walked outside. I heard their bikes rev up and then peel out.

I looked at Val and said, "Okay, well, I have an idea where we can leave Doc and Fido while we're on our honeymoon. Let's just get settled in here for now. Should I carry you across the threshold?"

She just smirked. After I unlocked the door, Val picked *me* up and carried me inside my little apartment, now her new home. Ivar was still there, right where I'd left him. The place had obviously been tossed, but my DVD collection was untouched, thank God. No more LPs and 45s, though, and Val had left all of hers with Phantasia back in their Mexico City house. I wondered if Val already missed it, given the relative squalor of her new home.

I pointed at Ivar, formally introducing him to my wife, though I still suspected they secretly knew each other. "Just like the one in your house in Mexico and at the lab in Costa Rica," I said, studying Val's face for a telling reaction.

"I never saw anything like that before," she said, straight-faced. "It's hideous!" Then she let Doc out of his crate, I set Fido down, and they began running around, playing. I fed Doc and realized I had no dog food for Fido, so I gave him some refried beans, which he devoured. I no longer trusted any brand of dog food, anyway. I was even going to start feeding Doc something else, maybe fresh fish. Nothing seemed safe anymore. Only one way to ignore it.

"Where do we sleep?" Val asked after giving the little place a quick once-over.

"Here," I said, pulling down the Murphy bed.

She smiled and began taking off her clothes. Then she

laid herself on the creaky, bumpy mattress, spread-eagle and ready.

I removed my clothes, climbed in next to her, and we began passionately making out. I couldn't believe this goddess, this Ultimate Female, was all mine.

Neither could my cock. It remained limp as overcooked linguini no matter how much Val tugged and sucked on it. It didn't help that Doc and Fido kept jumping on the bed, trying to horn in on the action.

"What the hell?" Val finally said, exasperated. "I thought you were some kind of sex expert?"

"No, not a sexpert, just an enthusiast," I said. "Though I guess my enthusiasm has been curbed."

"I'm in my forties, Vic. I'm at my sexual peak."

"I hit mine in my late teens and twenties. And thirties and forties. I was able to stretch it out a few decades, mostly by keeping my engine running by jerking off so much. Now I guess I've finally run out of fuel. Not even fumes left in my tank. I know, bad timing. Sorry. It's Nature's fault, not mine."

She just got up and took a shower. I just lay there, trying to revive Little Elvis, fantasizing about my old standby, Bettie Page, but no dice. Then I tried other old reliable images, like Caroline Munro in 1978's *Starcrash*, Still nothing.

"Maybe you should've saved those pictures of us from the first time," I said when Val came out, toweling her long hair, dripping wet. "That might inspire me."

"No," she said with a sigh. "I'm afraid it was the same even then. That's really why I deleted the pictures. There was no point in preserving a failed attempt for posterity, especially after waiting twenty-five years."

I sat up. "What? I couldn't even get it up the time I can't remember either?"

"No, Vic. I assumed it was due to the drugs. And maybe it still is, a side effect of impotence."

"Damn, don't even say that word!"

She leaned over and pulled my limp dick and said, "What else would you call this?"

"Maybe, like you suggest, the side effects are still lingering," I said. "By the time we get to Hawaii, I'll be back at full power. You just watch. And this really will be our first time!"

She nodded, unconvinced, then rolled over and fell asleep.

I finally found my true love, and I couldn't get it up anymore. What a time for Little Elvis to actually die. He'd faked it a few times, but now it seemed permanent. I thought: what would Dr. Nick do?, and was considering Viagra as a possible solution, but frankly, after Hal exposed this global corporate conspiracy against consumers, I was wary of any medications from now on. Or any processed food.

That night we lay in each other's arms, uncertain of our future as a couple, since Val required satisfaction, and if her lawfully wedded husband couldn't give it to her, Phantasia or somebody else would, in a heartbeat. But not even that prospect revived my libido.

While she slept, I just lay there wide awake, thinking about the possible fate of the real Fido, as well as the departed souls of Laura, Jade, Dianne, Fifi, and even Hal. Maybe they were all hanging out with Doc and Raven in some celestial Utopia. Or not. Where the hell did all these people keep going, anyway?

Finally I drifted off into semi-slumber, only to be abruptly awakened by what I groggily perceived to be the fluttering of wings. Bat wings. Then I turned and saw Val just getting back into bed.

"What are you doing?" I asked her.

"I had to use your bathroom," she said sleepily.

"You mean *our* bathroom," I said, but she didn't respond. She was already asleep again.

The next morning we left for Portland in my Corvair, which fortunately was parked out front, as Jade promised, but with tons of tickets on the windshield. I was lucky it hadn't been impounded yet, but maybe that was because I was still considered a hero to the local cops. We took Doc and Fido with us. I'd decided to leave them with Monica and Maria while we were in Hawaii. Plus I wanted to tell Monica in person about Val, especially since at one point, we thought we'd be married to each other by now, if only by default.

"You should've called first!" Monica said, happily surprised, opening the door wearing nothing but a bathrobe, which seemed to be the way all women greeted me lately. A stunningly gorgeous black woman who resembled Haji from the Russ Meyer movies (at least the eyes, hair, lips, and tits) came out from behind her, wearing nothing but a towel, fresh from the shower.

"I wanted you to be the first to meet my wife," I said as Val hugged them both a little too long.

"Good, now you can meet mine too," Monica said, indicating Maria, whom I'd heard much about, but never actually met in person. They both flashed their rocks at us. We flashed our pebbles right back. Of course, their stones were bigger and more expensive than ours, which Val had purchased from a kiosk at a mall complex called The Galleria back down in Houston, on the cheap, but then we were in a hurry to get out of Texas ASAP. Too fucking hot.

"Nice of you to tell me," I said to Monica, hugging her.

"I was waiting for the right moment, and this is it," she said, squeezing me tight.

"Congratulations," I said sincerely.

"Likewise, Vic. You've been yearning for stability since I've known you. Even more than me."

"Doc is happy for us," I whispered in her ear. "The dude, not the cat."

"Both," she whispered back.

Then we wiped away each other's tears and sat down to coffee and Blue Star Doughnuts.

"I understand why you named your cat Doc," Monica said to me. "But is Fido the best name you could think of for the dog? Not very original."

"It's not like the dog name, it's after the Canadian zombie movie, 'Fido.'" I said, reveling in my own cleverness. "Because that's the name of the pet zombie in the movie."

"Yes, but that title was still taken from the tired old generic dog name," Monica said.

"Well, it's a twist on a twist."

"Hey, how did you like Costa Rica?" Maria asked, abruptly changing the subject. "Monica and I have always wanted to go there."

I shook my head in disgust. "Nothing but relentless heat, bugs, and zombies."

Val nudged me. "It's a beautiful place," she said.

"Zombies?" Maria said. "Like on 'The Walking Dead'?"

"Figure of speech," I said quickly. "It's just how I see people nowadays."

"Still the misanthrope," Monica observed.

"More than ever."

"But what about the flora and fauna?" Maria asked. "And the wildlife and the sun?"

"I didn't really notice the animals except when some tried to eat me. As far as trees go, I'll take evergreens over palms any day. And fuck the sun. I hate that giant flaming turd."

Val rolled her eyes.

"So where are you two off to next?" Monica asked.

"Hawaii," Val said. "You know, because we hate the sun."

"Maria and I went there for our honeymoon, too," Monica said.

"Which island?" Val asked.

"Kauai."

"That's on our itinerary, too."

"That's where Elvis got married in 'Blue Hawaii'!" I pointed out.

"The real reason we chose it," Val said. "Or rather, I did."

Monica looked at Val, then at me, and said, "Wow. You really are a perfect match."

There was an uncomfortable pause, then I said: "Hey, I got an idea! What about you all engage in a threesome while I watch?"

They all laughed, but stopped when they realized I wasn't kidding.

"I don't think that would be appropriate," Maria said.

"I agree," Monica said. "Shame on you, Vic."

Val just smiled, but said nothing. Damn. She would've totally gone for it, I bet. Maybe later.

After more catching-up chit-chat we went for a walk on Hawthorne Avenue, just down the block from their house, which they owned (unlike me, Monica invested her share of The Drive-Inn sale). We caught a movie (*Wonder Woman*; love Gal Gadot but my heart still belongs to Lynda Carter) with dinner at the Bagdad Theater, then browsed around Powell's Bookstore across the street. It felt strange. After a while, nobody had much to say to the other. We were on a double date, but mostly just stuck to our assigned partners. I guess Monica and I were afraid of a back-slide into our complicated history. Or at least I was. I often thought I should've just married her. But now I'd lost my chance. I had Val, though, and that felt right, except for the unplanned celibacy part. I never had that problem with Monica, or any woman, for that matter. The irony was killing me.

Waking from another sadly sexless night, Val restlessly tossing in her sleep with frustration, we flew early the next morning to Honolulu where we stayed at the Royal Hawaiian Hotel on Waikiki Beach, all on Val's dime, since she offered and I was broke. Plus half of her ill-gotten gains were now legally mine, anyway.

Since it was so warm and sunny there, being a tropical island and all, we hardly left our hotel, especially since we'd had enough of that crap in Costa Rica. Val just lay quietly in the plush bed, channel surfing mindlessly. The scenery was gorgeous outside out window, though.

One local news station reported how Hawaii was preparing for a potential nuclear attack from North Korea. Meanwhile, back home in Seattle, smoke from wildfires raging all across British Columbia was drifting down to Seattle, engulfing it in a hot, smoggy haze, much like a nuclear winter. Or how I imagined one would be. I think nuclear winters are actually cold. The way things were heading, I'd find out. The hard way.

There was no escaping the outside world, not even here in our honeymoon haven; no completely safe sanctuary from all the sadness and madness. Only temporary, illusionary refuge, culled from escapist entertainment. And each other.

So instead of the news, we binge-watched the first two seasons of *Ash vs. Evil Dead*, a show I'd been meaning to catch up on. She wasn't that crazy about it, but I loved it. After that she made me watch *RuPaul's Drag Race*. We were even. Well, I thought so, anyway.

But no sex. Even here in Hawaii, the site of his namesake's biggest concert, Little Elvis still refused to perform. He had lapsed into a terminal coma. Val just slept and ate. I just wanted to find the local tiki bar and drink.

Ironically, none of the locals in Hawaii had any idea what I meant when I asked, "Where's the nearest tiki bar?" There were tiki statues all over the island, some in bars, even. But the term "tiki bar" seemed foreign to them. I guess their idea of "exotic" was something quintessentially mainland. Like me.

Finally, in a little alley off Kalakaua Ave., I came upon what appeared to be a speakeasy. Those were trendy back on the mainland, so I guess it made sense they'd have them here, too. The only indication was a glowing neon tiki above a locked door.

I knocked and a panel slid open and a silky voice asked for the password. I didn't know it, so I just said, "Aloha," and the door opened right up. Basically all you had to do was make one up on the spot and if they liked it, you were in. The bouncer was actually a really foxy barefoot *wahine* wearing nothing but a flower pattern sarong. The interior was very dark and cool and densely decorated with Polynesian Pop Art. My kind of place.

Not only was this an "authentic" tiki bar, but the bartender was wearing a fez hat. I sat on a stool as Arthur Lyman music played from the sound system and *Gidget Goes Hawaiian* played silently on a TV behind the bar. It was almost like a tiki version of The Drive-Inn. Suddenly I missed Doc. The human one. And the feline one, too. In fact, despite my beautiful bride back in our hotel bed, I felt lonelier than ever, only because I was finally so close to true happiness, close enough to literally touch it, and have it touch me back, but it remained just out of reach.

The bartender looked vaguely familiar. He introduced himself as Jason. I struck up a conversation with him, and he reminded me of where I knew him from: Tacoma Cabana, back by Puget Sound. He'd just opened yet another tiki bar right up the street from there, called Devil's Reef, which I planned to check out when I got back home. Jason was also co-owner of this joint, which was called Oahu Ohana. He was in town to help out while his partner Robyn was away on business.

Anyway, inspired by the sordid events that took place at his Tacoma joint during my visit there with Raven and Charlie, Jason had actually created a cocktail in my honor.

It was called "Every Woman I Love Is Undead." He thought I'd be back to Tacoma Cabana someday, but instead, I wound up here. We toasted the synchronicity.

I took a sip of his concoction and tasted blissful nectar. It was perfect. "Brother, you have no idea how much I need this, or how ironically ideal that name is."

"I have a pretty good idea," he said cryptically.

It was then I noticed Ivar, or his demonic stalker facsimile, sitting on the shelf behind Jason, amid some tiki statues and tiki mugs. Instead of asking Jason if he saw it too, and had planted it there on purpose, I did my best to ignore the damn thing. I was convinced he'd be following me wherever I went for the rest of my life, so I might as well just accept it.

I finished my cocktail, then Jason made me another, and another. Besides Arthur Lyman, Jason's exotica music mix included some of my personal favorites, relatively obscure classics like "Taboo" by the South Sea Serenaders and "Moon Mist" by The Out-Islanders. I never wanted to leave. But I had to face reality sometime, and the fact was, despite the apocalyptic nature of the world in general these days, my personal life was better than ever, hampered only by my sudden lack of virility.

Finally I bid Jason good night, or he just politely cut me off, and I stumbled back onto the moonlit street, bumping into tourists, until I found my way back to the Pink Palace.

Val was sleeping naked in bed. The TV was on. She'd selected a *XXX-rated movie inspired by the 1960s Batman* TV show, still one of my favorites. Meaning the original series, not the porn knockoff, though that looked good, too, from what I saw of it. My childhood hero Adam West was now as dead as my dick, though. I felt so depressed, more so than usual. I popped a Xanax—the one type of drug I didn't want to give up, no matter how secretly tainted it may have been—and then lay next to her, gazing in awe at her curvaceous beauty, which still failed to stimulate my senses beyond the appreciation of natural beauty, until I finally fell asleep.

I had wet nightmares about Laura and Jade and Dianne rising from the dead as rotting, EC Comics-style zombies, but still pretty sexy, all naked and dead, attacking me in this very hotel room, fucking and eating my brains out, like a scene from *Cemetery Man (Dellamorte Dellamore),* one of my all-time favorites.

When I unwillingly woke up from this dream in the middle of the night (or maybe it was day, hard to tell with the shades drawn all the time), I went straight into another one, or so it seemed.

Val was on top of me, sucking on my neck with her tongue and teeth. I thought she was just giving me a hickey, until she sat up and wiped quite a bit of my blood from her face, as some trickled down her tits. I licked my blood off her nipples. It was right out of a 1970s Hammer lesbian vampire movie or a classic *giallo,* or better yet, the lurid cover of a *fumetti,* which were erotic horror comics popular in Italy in the 1970s and '80s. Two of my favorite artists in that particular field were Emanuele Taglietti and Alessandro Biffignandi, and even they couldn't have painted this vision any better. It was right out of my deepest, darkest sexual fantasy.

Plus she was my *wife*.

I suddenly felt a familiar stirring in my groin. Then I noticed Little Elvis was ready to rock, rising for the grave for his big comeback special.

As if in a sensual trance, Val kissed her way down my quivering torso and took my suddenly rock-hard cock in her mouth and sucked the semen right out of it. Then she mounted me and sucked my neck harder and harder as she came, and I came again.

Now *this* was a honeymoon. Well worth the quarter century wait, too. Actually, I'd been waiting for this very moment my entire life, or most of it. I wanted to relish it for all it was worth.

Suffice it to say, we didn't get any sleep that night, and we even turned off the TV, at least for a while.

The next morning we went downstairs to the Mai Tai Bar on the beach, in full, glorious view of Diamondhead, which I'd previously only seen in movies and TV shows, and had a delicious breakfast, including Mai Tais served in real, carved out pineapple shells. Next we walked down the beach to Duke's for more cocktails, then moseyed around Waikiki a bit, absorbing the aloha atmosphere. But then, despite the trade winds, it got too damn hot, so we returned to our air-conditioned cave and fucked some more. My neck was covered in hickeys, all purple and bruised. Val was literally sucking me dry. And I didn't care. I was her love slave for life. And beyond.

We cancelled our planned plane hop over to Kauai once we discovered the resort where Elvis got married in *Blue Hawaii,* the Coco Palms, was closed for good. No point. Other than brief breakfast trips to Leonard's Bakery for *malasadas,* sushi runs down to King Street, happy hour with Jason at Oahu Oahana, and sunset dinners at La Mariana Sailing Club, which had a blind piano player, we mainly spent our Hawaiian honeymoon indoors, making up for lost time. Fortunately thunderstorms raged outside for much of it, adding a gothic touch to our tropical vacation. Besides Raquel Welch, Val now reminded me of Helga Liné in Amando De Ossorio's 1974 monster-mermaid masterpiece *The Loreley's Grasp*, which only made me love and desire and appreciate her that much more.

Besides sex, we binge-watched the original *Hawaii Five-O* with Jack Lord, though we fucked and slept through at least half the episodes. Neither of us had ever been to Hawaii and we hardly saw any of it while there, other than the vintage scenery on our TV screen. But it didn't matter. Mission accomplished. I'd found myself again.

"Why do you think it took me so long?" I asked my live-in shrink. "Fear of commitment?"

"Partly. You were afraid to fall in love with me."

"You weren't?"

"I'm not afraid of anything, Vic."

I waited, but it took a little while longer to hear the words I really wanted from her.

Our last night there, Val, following a particularly loud and intense orgasm, finally whispered in my ear, "I love you."

"I never thought I'd hear you say it," I said.

"I never planned to. That wasn't part of our original deal, way back when. Consider it a bonus."

"I didn't plan on falling in love with you, either."

"No, but I knew you would. One reason I was hesitant to get in touch with you and fulfill our contract."

"Oh, you did? How did you know that?"

"I'm your ideal woman."

"Well, yes. Hell, yes. You certainly are. Am I your ideal man?"

"I don't have ideals. Not anymore. But if I did, you'd set the standard."

Then she bit the hell out of my neck again. I smiled as she sucked my blood, and various other bodily fluids. I totally and completely belonged to my quasi-lesbian *lucha* semi-vampire with an authentic PhD. And she belonged to me. Forever. Or close enough.

"If that movie of my life had been made, I'd never have become a dog walker, and then I'd have never have found you," I said.

"I already knew where you were, though," she said. "I was just biding my time."

"I'm a lousy detective, aren't I?"

"Yes, but a terrific lover."

"And dog walker."

"No. You're a terrible dog walker. That's one reason

you're here with me now."

"Well, I only do it for the exercise now anyway, since I'm a kept man. I'm finally making a living with my natural talent. I'm not a good dick, but I *have* a good dick."

She was already asleep again. Or pretending to be. She did that a lot.

I realized I knew next to nothing about her background, or her extended family. She never mentioned them, and frankly, I didn't care, because it didn't matter. I was her family now. We were both starting over halfway through life, fresh as Costa Rican tropical passion fruit picked right off the tree.

Speaking of which, after we got back home in Seattle, we received a package from the Melrost Airport Bed and Breakfast down in Alajeula, the temporary home base of the Writers' Colony of San Buenas until construction of the new buildings was completed. Inside the package was a framed, signed 8x10 photo of Brett and his first writers' retreat attendees, which included all of our old pals from Casa de la Gata: Tim, Roy, Zeke, Carl Sloane, and Justin with his new Filipino boyfriend, Fernando. Even Molly and Curt were there! They had all decided to become writers after their shared experiences under the wicked spell of Hal and his evil, mysterious drug that the world would never hear about, which was a good thing, though I got no official credit for stopping it. Well, with a little help from my friends.

Noticeably absent from the photo was Phantasia. Though I did notice one bat clinging to the wall just behind the group.

The irony, of course, was that however inadvertently, Hal's posthumously laundered dirty money made it all possible. The world works in mysterious ways. It seems the most crucial mysteries in life are not meant to be solved. So why even fucking bother? Being a detective was pointless, especially for someone like me that was totally clueless, anyway. I'm better off picking up puppy poop for chump change. At least that has some sort of routine resolution.

Shortly after we returned from our honeymoon to our cozy little home, where we continued to lie in bed and fuck and watch TV, I was channel surfing as my wife—my *wife*—slept by my side. I stopped when I saw the word "ZOMBIES!" behind some talking head spewing an editorial. The topic was the rapidly growing opioid epidemic, and how if it wasn't contained soon, a dangerously large portion of the population could become "zombified" addicts and actually pose a threat to society at large. I got a chill, and I kept flipping.

Another talking head was reporting about mysteriously tainted alcohol down in Mexico, causing tourists to become ill and sometimes even black out. I guess the "social experiments" were being continued without Hal, but by someone else. His legacy lived on. But me? Been there, done that. I kept flipping.

On the next channel I saw footage of the latest terrorist attack in Paris, a city I'd love to visit someday, since I figured it would actually be worth leaving my house again. Not at the moment, though. Anyway, a reporter was relating news about the tragedy when I saw two women sitting at a table together in a cafe. They were making out. Then suddenly they both looked at the camera, waved, and threw kisses. At me, it seemed.

I could've sworn it was Jade and Laura.

But then they started making out again, and I couldn't see their faces clearly. I jumped out of bed and tried to get a better look, but the camera had panned away by then. Completely startled, I tried waking up Val to tell her, but to no avail. When I told her at breakfast, she just laughed, especially when I said I suspected a secret society of super-intelligent bi-sexual vampire women co-existed on this planet, and I'd married into their ranks. I was just glad they were on my side, or I was on their's, anyway.

Instead of blood, or just blood, they apparently subsisted on semen, like Lina Romay in Jess Franco's 1975 classic *Female Vampire*, or even the savage suburban swingers in 1973's equally essential *Invasion of the Bee Girls*. This would also explain, at least to my satisfaction, why these women were so anxious to get me into bed and drain me of my precious bodily fluids. Val didn't confirm or deny my theory, but that would be the only rational explanation for Jade and Laura rising from the dead like that, then relocating to Paris. Anything seemed possible at this point.

I mean, after all, I was now actually *married* to The Phone Phantom, someone I didn't even believe truly existed until she revealed her true identity as my true love, many years after the fact. What were the odds? There just had to be some ironic order to the Universe. Or at the very least it had a healthy sense of humor. At my expense, anyway.

Later, Monica and Maria drove Doc and Fido back up to us, then we all went out to an expensive dinner at Canlis, a fancy Rat Pack-style restaurant, before returning to their room at the Hotel Ballard right around the corner from my pad and having a four way. Just kidding. Maybe. You'll never know for sure. And neither will I. I think Val has already proven to you that I'm an unreliable narrator.

The morning after our alleged orgy, I took my girls out to lunch at a great Puerto Rican restaurant in my neighborhood of Ballard, called La Isla. Being Puerto Rican herself, by way of New York City, Maria especially loved it. (I thought she was Cuban till Monica corrected me). I scored some points with my sister-in-law (meaning she's not a blood relative, for the record), at least until I started serenading her with the song "Maria" from *West Side Story* and Monica ("I guess the makes you Tony") kicked me under the table.

My savings had finally run out, but Val had been

stashing loot she stole from Hal for years. That's what funded our honeymoon, and now our married life. We were rich. No more dog-walking for me. Except for Fido, of course. Unless the KGB put a hit out on me, the future looked very bright indeed. Or even better, dark 'n' stormy.

In fact, as I write this, it's a rainy autumn day. Mrs. Valentine and I are enjoying champagne and oysters (a proven aphrodisiac, just in case Little Elvis decides to fake his death again) at Frank's on 55th in the Bryant neighborhood. Robert Mitchum's *Calypso Is Like So* album is playing over the sound system, or at least that's what I hear. I only had one glass of champagne. Maybe two. In any case, I actually felt something like unfiltered, unadulterated happiness for the first time in a long time, maybe ever. And it had nothing to do with alcohol or sex or B movies and everything to do with my wife, my family, and my best friend in the world, Dr. Mrs. Esmeralda Ava Margarita Valentina Valdez Valentine, PhD.

I guess sometimes you can teach an old dog new tricks.

MR. AND MRS. VALENTINE WILL RETURN

Made in the USA
San Bernardino, CA
06 September 2017